Hilltop Lodge Christmas

Hilltop Lodge Christmas

Book Two

D. Kay Taylor, Ph.D.

Copyright © 2020 by D. Kay Taylor, Ph.D.
Cover Illustration by Tara B. Taylor

Library of Congress Control Number:	2019920654
ISBN: Hardcover	978-1-7960-7798-8
Softcover	978-1-7960-7797-1
eBook	978-1-7960-7796-4

All rights reserved. No part of this book may be reproduced or transmitted in any form or by any means, electronic or mechanical, including photocopying, recording, or by any information storage and retrieval system, without permission in writing from the copyright owner.

This is a work of fiction. Names, characters, places and incidents either are the product of the author's imagination or are used fictitiously, and any resemblance to any actual persons, living or dead, events, or locales is entirely coincidental.

Any people depicted in stock imagery provided by Getty Images are models, and such images are being used for illustrative purposes only.
Certain stock imagery © Getty Images.

Print information available on the last page.

Rev. date: 01/03/2020

To order additional copies of this book, contact:
Xlibris
1-888-795-4274
www.Xlibris.com
Orders@Xlibris.com
802267

Dedicated to my sister, Linda McGrain Holiday, who instilled in me a passion to learn about our Irish family history. This story—although fiction—is based on real characters and events. In this novel a young man named Patrick—son of a poor farmer—perchance crosses paths with Frances Dodge—the daughter (and heir) of John Dodge (co-founder of the Dodge Motor Company). Although these two young people hail from very different worlds—they nonetheless share some striking similarities—and a genuine bond of friendship takes root. This juxtaposition guides the story line.

D. Kay Taylor

CONTENTS

PROLOGUE ix

Chapter 1 Making a List 1
Chapter 2 Holiday Shopping 35
Chapter 3 Decorating Hilltop 55
Chapter 4 Visiting Rose Terrace 83
Chapter 5 Holiday Luncheon 103
Chapter 6 Christmas Day 123

PROLOGUE[1]

This book series explores the first year in a young girl's life—Frances Dodge—who was the daughter of auto baron John Dodge—as she experiences adolescence at Meadow Brook Farm and her own Hilltop Lodge following the tragic events surrounding the loss of her father, her uncle and her sister. After the untimely deaths of John and Horace Dodge, Frances' mother and aunt became heirs to one of the largest fortunes in America. In Book One (Hilltop Lodge: Frances' Birthday), the reader learns how her mother and aunt sold the Dodge Brothers Motor Car Company in 1925 for an astounding $146 million—her mother's remarriage to lumber baron Alfred G. Wilson—and their permanent move to the 1500-acre Meadow Brook Farm. Here they lived in a large farm

---

[1] *Book One Hilltop Lodge: Frances' Birthday Celebration; en.wikipdeia.org*

house for three years while Mrs. Dodge Wilson worked with the renowned Detroit architectural firm of Smith, Hinchman & Grylls to design and build an expansive, spectacular mansion—Meadow Brook Hall.

Meadow Brook Hall featured elaborately carved wood and stone, handmade hardware and ceramic art tiles, intricately molded and carved plaster ceilings, ornately carved beams, gargoyles, hidden stairways, stained glass window insets, crystal and art glass lighting fixtures, gold-plated bathroom fittings, twenty-six bedrooms (each with a built-in safe) and twenty-four individually designed fireplaces. Mrs. Dodge Wilson devoted countless hours—years, really—to furnishing and decorating Meadow Brook Hall. It was her passion. And indeed, it was—and is—a grand hall.

The Dodge-Wilson home would later be referred to as one of American's "castles", boasting 110 rooms covering 88,000 square feet. Before their deaths, Mr. and Mrs. Wilson had arranged to give their estate, mansion and property to Michigan State University to be developed into a college. It is now Oakland University that maintains the hall and grounds. But Meadow Brook Hall is only the backdrop of the story series. Readers will learn about the wonderful—and magical—events that took place in a 6-room, 750-square-foot residence—Knole Cottage. Originally named Hilltop Lodge, it was designed to be a playhouse for Frances (although she was already twelve years of age) where she could learn the skills of managing a household. But it was so much, much more.

Frances loved Meadow Brook Farm—and Hilltop Lodge—for so many reasons. But most importantly, here is where she would first learn to love and ride horses. Later, Frances would become an internationally famous horsewoman. She bred and raced horses and set a record for time in the saddle at the Red Mile in Kentucky that stood for fifty-four years. (This record was broken by her daughter!) Book One told the events surrounding her birthday celebration at Meadow Brook in her Hilltop Lodge. Book Two relates the story of her first Christmas here.

Chapter 1
Making a List

Wednesday, December 1, 1926

It wasn't until Frances had met with her tutor, Miss Taylor, at 9 a.m. to begin her morning lessons that she realized that today marked the beginning of the month of December! There had been so much commotion during the final week of November that she completely forgot that December had arrived! Yes—those last days in November had indeed been quite eventful—with her family celebrating both the Thanksgiving holiday and her twelfth birthday—as well as Frances' first overnight party in her own spectacular playhouse (and, of course, her surprise meeting with Patrick at her Hilltop Lodge).

The two-hour morning lesson seemed to especially drag today. Frances feigned interest in the classes—for in truth the only subject that really inspired Frances was horses. And although her mother—Mrs. Matilda Dodge Wilson—supported her love of riding and training—she also insisted that women devote significant effort to obtaining a formal education. So Frances tried to focus on today's lesson. When Miss Taylor dismissed Frances at 11 a.m. she reminded her, "I will see you again at two o'clock!"

Frances bounced up the stairs to her bedroom. Now only 23 days remained until Christmas Eve! She had so much planning to do! Frances sat at the desk in her bedroom—staring at a blank sheet of lined paper—with the exception of the words 'Christmas List' that she had scribbled at the top of the sheet 10 minutes earlier. She sat motionless—uncertain where best to begin her list. A knock at her bedroom door broke her stagnant trance.

"Come in." she cheerfully shouted. Frances turned in her chair to see that it was her mother. She stood and walked to her. "Mother—I'm so happy to see you. I could use your help. You are the best at planning and organizing."

Mrs. Dodge Wilson embraced her daughter. "Of course, Frances—I am always here for you. And I also wanted to ask about your help with something." She motioned for Frances to return to her desk chair while she pulled the room's upholstered chair closer to the desk. They arranged the chairs so that they sat face-to-face.

"Now—how might I help you?" her mother asked.

Frances hesitated. "But, mother, you approached me first—so you should have the first opportunity to ask me for help." Frances was very curious as to what type of help her mother might want from her. It made her feel so grownup—so much like an adult—that her mother was seeking advice from her.

Mrs. Dodge Wilson smiled widely as she reflected on how well her daughter was maturing. Frances was learning how to set aside her own wants and needs—to focus more on others. "Thank you, Frances. I wanted to ask for your assistance in planning a surprise birthday luncheon celebration for your stepfather. He will be 43 years old on December 15th."

Forty-three sounded terribly old to twelve-year-old Frances. "When was he born?" she asked.

"The same year that I was born—in 1883." her mother responded.

"So—you are as old as stepfather?" Frances was somewhat startled. Her stepfather had quite a bit of gray hair. She just assumed that he was much older than her mother. Frances didn't like to think of her mother as being 'old'. Old age was linked to death—and Frances still harbored fears of losing those closest to her. The early loss of her father, uncle and sister had triggered these fears. Frances' now looked alarmed.

Mrs. Dodge Wilson could not control her laughter, but managed to say, "I am actually older than Alfred—but only by two months. But I might add—forty-three is not all that ancient."

Frances felt certain that her face had grown very red in color. She was embarrassed that her questions had seemed to suggest that her mother was old. This was not a perception appreciated by most women.

But her mother leaned forward in her chair and grasped Frances' hands in her own. "It's quite okay, Frances. It's all a matter of perspective. When I was your age—I believed my parents to be almost archaic."

They laughed together. This shared laughter relaxed Frances—allowing her to return to the business at hand.

Her mother added, "I was thinking that a luncheon could be planned for our 'older' friends, and then also a family dinner."

Frances chuckled at the age reference, but proceeded to offer her thoughts on the birthday celebration. "Well…the 15th is exactly two weeks from today. But if you wanted to plan a surprise luncheon party for your friends, perhaps you could celebrate on the Saturday before his birthday?" On December 11th?" Frances was studying the calendar sheet that was on her desk next to her 'empty' Christmas list. "How about Jacoby's German Biergarten restaurant?"

Mrs. Dodge Wilson looked quizzically at her young daughter. "Frances—I think that a luncheon in Detroit would be very nice—but how do you know about Biergarten's?" she asked.

"I read an article in the newspaper." Frances announced with an air of exaggerated casualness. "It has been a favorite in Detroit for more than 20 years. And because of our German heritage, I thought that this might be a good choice." Mrs. Dodge Wilson now reflected on how Frances was also becoming adept at planning and organizing. She was pleased that her daughter was 'absorbing' some of her best qualities.

"Well...I'll be going into Detroit on Saturday for a meeting with Mr. William Kapp, the lead architect for Meadow Brook Hall...so I could make the arrangements with a restaurant at that time. I will certainly look into Biergarten's—and a few others."

Frances felt pleased that she could help her mother. But she also wanted to insure that she and her brother Danny would also be a part of celebrating stepfather's birthday. "And we can still plan a dinner and cake here at home on his actual birthday so that Danny and I can join in the celebration!"

"Of course!" her mother replied. "Now...what can I help you with?"

"I wanted to ask you about my Christmas shopping list. First—I want to make sure that I don't forget anyone. Second—I thought that you might have some ideas about gifts that you could share with me."

Mrs. Dodge Wilson noted the empty sheet on Frances' desk. "I'll wait while you jot down the names for your gift list."

Frances wrote frantically—as she didn't want her mother to wait too long. She divided the list into three sections: family, staff, and horses. Frances chuckled as she drafted the final category. She expected that her mother would find humor in her formal designation of 'horses' on her Christmas list.

CHRISTMAS LIST

<u>Family</u>
- Mother
- Stepfather
- Brother - Danny

<u>Staff</u>
- Miss Taylor *tutor*
- Nanny Mary *nanny*
- Anne *housekeeper*
- Hannah *cook*
- Hank *stables*
- John *grounds/driver*
- George *farm hand*

<u>Horses</u>
- Dolly
- Duke

Frances turned her chair back around to again face her mother as she triumphantly handed her the finished list. But as she watched her mother read the gift inventory—she didn't see her mother display any humor. Actually, her mother appeared to be a bit uneasy. This confused Frances. At last her mother looked up and spoke.

"Well…I didn't realize that you would want to purchase gifts for the house and grounds staff." Mrs. Dodge Wilson looked skeptical. "I'm not certain if that would be a good idea."

"But Mother—I want to show them how much I appreciate what they do."

"I understand your feelings—and it is very considerate of you to want to recognize their work here at Meadow Brook Farm. But your stepfather and I plan to give a Christmas bonus to each employee."

Frances hesitated—and then asked, "What is a bonus?"

Her mother responded, "It is a cash gift."

Frances' disappointment was obvious to her mother, but she remained silent. Her mother continued.

"I would approve of you purchasing perhaps a small gift for both your teacher and your nanny." Her mother then added, "And if you want to select a greeting card for each house staff member—I think that would be nice."

Mrs. Dodge Wilson surveyed her daughter's face—trying to see if her suggestions were satisfactory or not. But she wasn't able to fully read her facial expression. Finally her mother said, "Frances—receiving personal gifts in addition to a cash bonus may create an awkward situation. It may cause the staff to feel uncomfortable—as they may feel obligated to reciprocate."

This explanation alarmed Frances. "Oh, mother, I didn't expect any gifts in return."

"I know that—but it might be confusing for some of our staff. Do you understand?" Mrs. Dodge Wilson wanted to confirm that Frances accepted her mother's advisement. Her mother was also thinking ahead—when Meadow Brook Hall would be completed—the number of staff would increase greatly. It just wouldn't be feasible for her daughter to purchase individual gift items for each staff person.[2]

Frances again hesitated—but then replied in a dry, repetitive manner, "I would like to buy something small for

---

[2] The number of staff would grow to forty.

Miss Taylor and for Nanny Mary—that's all." She then arose from her chair, bent over her mother, and kissed her cheek—thus signaling her apparent acceptance of the situation.

"I would also suggest that you write down more than one item for each family member on your list. We can shop together—and I can help you decide!"

When her mother departed her room, Frances pulled another sheet of paper from her desk drawer. This would be her 'secret' Christmas list. "I will select something for Anne, Hannah, Hank, John and George—but I will make sure that they do not know that I am the giver!" Frances announced aloud. And then it struck her—another name to add to her secret list—Patrick!

At noon, Frances descended the stairs to the dining room. Today her stepfather joined the family for lunch—as he had no other business obligations this afternoon. Frances was happy to see him at the table—as she planned to ask him for his Christmas wish list.

Following the recitation of grace Frances asked, "Stepfather—I am gathering ideas for my holiday shopping list—and I wondered if you would share with me some things that you might want."

Without hesitation Danny interjected, "I know what I want."

Mrs. Dodge Wilson smiled patiently as she reminded Danny that it was impolite to interrupt. "Danny—your sister has posed a question to your stepfather. Please wait until he has answered."

It can be very difficult to be patient when you are nine years old—especially when the discussion involves Christmas presents, but Danny mumbled that he was sorry and sat still.

Mr. Wilson reached over to Danny and affectionately patted his right shoulder. "Don't worry. I promise that I won't take long to share my ideas."

"Frances—I feel that I am so very blessed to have your mother, you and your brother as my family—and to call Meadow Brook Farm our home. It would be difficult to ask for more than these blessings." Although this was a beautiful heartfelt declaration, Mr. Wilson perceived a hint of disappointment in Frances' expression—and so he continued. "But there are a few items that I could certainly use."

He now had Frances' full attention. "Yes—please share!" she pleaded.

"Well, I very much want to learn more about agriculture. I envision that Meadow Brook Farm could someday become something of a prominent breeding farm. So I would like to read as much as possible… some books on this topic…"[3]

Frances repeated, "Books. Okay. And what else?"

Mr. Wilson didn't wish to disappoint Frances, so he proceeded to add a few more items. "A new pair of winter gloves—lined—would be appreciated as the days are becoming increasingly colder. Or a new winter hat and scarf would also help to keep me warmer." He then scanned each of their faces—his eyes betraying a certain childlike mischief.

---

[3] Meadow Brook Farm would indeed become more than a 'working farm'. Mr. and Mrs. Dodge gradually acquired more land—building Meadow Brook into a 2,600 acre farm. It was described as one of the finest agricultural developments in the state, producing superior lines of pedigree livestock. The Wilsons became well known for their prize-winning purebred animals.

"And—I wouldn't turn down any of those Sander's chocolate candies if these appeared in my Christmas stocking."[4]

"Me, too—I want chocolate." Danny couldn't resist adding his approval to the final wish list item. But this time his mother did not admonish him about interrupting his stepfather—rather the entire table shared laughter.

Mrs. Dodge Wilson then added, "Me, too. I also enjoyed those chocolates that we purchased when Frances and I went birthday shopping in Detroit!"

"Okay…chocolate for everyone!" Frances announced with great certainty. "But what else would you like, Mother?"

---

[4] The Sander's Chocolate Company was founded by a Mr. Frederick Sanders Schmidt in June of 1875. (He was German born like Mrs. Dodge Wilson—but he used his middle name for his business.) He had first leased a small shop on Woodward Avenue when he began his business. By 1891, Mr. Sanders opened a new much larger building (also on Woodward Avenue) that he called 'The Pavilion of Sweets'. The auto pioneer Mr. Henry Ford actually worked for Sanders before forming his Ford Motor Company in 1903. Mr. Sanders hired Ford who was a young mechanic at the time working at the Thomas Edison Illuminating Company! The store was famous for ice cream sodas, fudge, and the Bumpy Cake.

Mrs. Dodge Wilson smiled. She leaned across the table and stroked Frances' hair. "Like your stepfather has expressed…I feel so very blessed to have this family and home. But I will share with you one request…although you cannot find it in a department store."

With this declaration, everyone at the table stopped eating. They stared at Mrs. Wilson awaiting her response. Frances was puzzled. "What is it, mother?" she asked.

Her mother sensed the anticipation or eagerness of her husband, daughter and son…and thus in a playful manner she delayed answering Frances. She tilted her head toward the ceiling—gazing as though she saw something there.

"Frances, I would like you to write me a short story about your Hilltop Lodge." With this declaration, Mrs. Dodge Wilson returned her admiring gaze to Frances. "You are such a clever writer."

Frances smiled. "Mother—I accept your challenge!"

Frances now turned her attention to Danny. "And what would you like in addition to chocolate?"

Danny quickly answered—rattling off a string of desired items. "I want a Lionel electric train set, a Coaster wagon, a fire engine, Tootsietoy cars, Lincoln logs, Tinkertoys, a _____."

His barrage of toy product names was disrupted by his mother. "Danny, that is quite enough. Please select just one or two of those items for your sister to shop for." Then in an effort to lift his spirits, she added, "Plus the chocolates, of course."

Following lunch, Frances returned to her bedroom. She again sat at her desk with her Christmas List. She added the following under Stepfather:

- Book about agriculture or farming
- Lined winter gloves
- Winter hat or scarf
- Sander's chocolates ★

Then she recorded the items that Danny had finally decided on:

- Lincoln logs
- Tinkertoys
- Sander's chocolates ★

And last—she recorded the unusual item requested by her mother—and, of course, the chocolates:

- ○ Short story about Hilltop Lodge
- ○ Sander's chocolates ★

She sketched a star next to the final item for each family member—as she wanted to make sure to buy some of these special chocolates. When Frances visited the famous Sander's Pavilion of Sweets in November with her mother—and was first greeted by the well-known red and white awning with its decorative tall spire (that Frances called a lighthouse tower and her mother corrected her and called it a 'minaret')—she couldn't wait to enter the legendary store on Woodward Avenue. Together they shopped the many aisles of chocolate treats, and then concluded their visit at the long service counter with low stools and bright red seats where they shared a hot fudge cream puff. Although it was delicious—this time when she visits the store, Frances would order an ice cream soda—Sander's signature item—as Mr. Sanders was credited with inventing the ice cream soda. SO—she made a mental note to include the Sander's Pavilion of Sweets on her Christmas shopping agenda.

She had completed her family list! She was making progress. But it was nearly 2 o'clock. Frances needed to return to her lessons. She would make sure to ask Miss Taylor about possible Christmas gifts. And before dinner, she could corner Nanny Mary and then Hannah. And tonight, following dinner, Frances would plead with her mother to allow her to visit her Hilltop Lodge for just half an hour or so. She was certain that Patrick would stop by when he saw the lights blazing. She especially was anxious to learn what item Patrick might want for Christmas.

Frances skipped down the stairs to the library to begin her afternoon schooling. Frances asked Miss Taylor if she could perhaps end their midday lessons a few minutes early today—as there was something important that she wished to discuss with her. Miss Taylor looked slightly amused, but responded, "Of course, Frances."

At 3:45 p.m., Miss Taylor closed her geography book and announced that the lesson was ended. She sat back in her chair in a relaxed pose. "Now...what would you like to talk about?" she asked.

Frances leaned forward in her chair—finding it difficult to contain her excitement. "I am composing my Christmas shopping list. Although it can be nice to surprise people, I want to be certain that I give you something that you would really treasure."

Miss Taylor was genuinely surprised by the question. "Frances—really—it isn't necessary for you to buy me a gift." But when she observed Frances' mood quickly change from enthusiasm to distress, she decided to oblige her request. "However, I am so touched by your thoughtfulness—and, yes—there is something that I have been wanting."

"What is it? Please tell me!" Frances' initial eagerness returned.

"Well—I really enjoy reading novels. I just finished a book that my sister Elizabeth loaned me, "The Great Gatsby" by Mr. Fitzgerald—which I did enjoy. But I haven't yet read, "Or So Big" by Edna Ferber—and her work was awarded the Pulitzer Prize in the novel category last year." Miss Taylor emphasized 'Pulitzer Prize'. "So...this is a gift that I would certainly treasure!"

Frances quickly calculated that both her stepfather and her tutor had selected a book—thus she would certainly make sure to include both the Sander's Pavilion of Sweets and a book store on her Christmas shopping trip agenda. "Thank you, Miss Taylor." Frances turned and exited the room with renewed purpose.

Frances found her mother waiting for her outside the door of the farmhouse 'library'. (It was really a smaller room adjacent to the dining room. The family would enjoy a true library when Meadowbrook Hall was completed!)

"Hello, Mother!" Frances said.

Mrs. Dodge Wilson appeared to be in a very pleasant mood, but when she told Frances that she wished to speak with her about her Christmas list—Frances felt a sudden sense of dread. Had her mother somehow learned about her secret gift list? Frances had placed this special paper separately from the list that her mother had approved—underneath some items in her bottom desk drawer. If her mother had found this list—not only would she know about Frances' plan to buy items for house staff—but her mother would not recognize the final name on the list: 'Patrick'.

"Let's return to your bedroom." Mrs. Dodge Wilson began to climb the stairs. Frances lagged behind her—apprehensive about this meeting.

They returned to the seats that they had occupied earlier in the day. Frances waited for her mother to begin.

"You look tense. Are you feeling well?" her mother asked.

Frances forced out the words, "Oh, yes. I'm fine. Just a little tired after my lessons."

Mrs. Dodge Wilson placed her hand on Frances' forehead. "No fever. Good!" And she continued. "I was thinking about your Christmas list—and I wanted to suggest another name."

Frances sudden dread was instantly relieved! Whew! "Who?" she asked.

"The family has been invited to a Christmas party on Saturday, December 18th at your Aunt Anna's home. Well…I suppose that it is now also the home of Mr. Dillman." her mother added.

Frances' Aunt Anna was the widow of her uncle Horace Dodge—her father's brother—the founders of the Dodge Motor Car Company. Both her father and uncle had died from the Spanish Flu when Frances was just five years old.[5] Her aunt had just recently remarried in May—just about six months ago—to a Mr. Hugh Dillman. He was an actor who was younger than her aunt (by 14 years!). She was 55—he was 41. People talked. But Frances didn't care about their age difference. She loved her Aunt Anna. They had married at her Rose Terrace mansion in Grosse Pointe, Michigan—a magnificent home that Anna and Horace had built in 1910.[6]

"I would love to visit Rose Terrace!" Frances exclaimed.

Her mother nodded. "So…perhaps you might want to bring a small gift for Anna and Hugh."

"Yes, I would." Frances added, "Thank you, mother."

Her mother then asked, "Would you like any suggestions for their gift?"

---

[5] The 1918-1920 flu pandemic was very deadly—killing 50 million people worldwide. It became known as the Spanish Flu because of its early death toll in Spain.

[6] Rose Terrace was a private home located at 12 Lakeshore Drive in Grosse Pointe Farms, Michigan. It was rebuilt in 1934 by Anna Dodge and her second husband Hugh Dillman.

"Oh, yes!" Frances responded. She was hoping to hear about some exotic, glamorous idea for the recent newlyweds.

Mrs. Dodge Wilson leaned toward her daughter and whispered, "Those special chocolates would be divine."

Frances' first reaction was one of slight exasperation. It seemed that candy was desired by almost everyone. But Frances projected a contented countenance—nodded her head in agreement—and playfully said, "Perhaps I will only need to shop at a single store—since everyone fancies those chocolates." She, of course, was only teasing her mother. It was a lighthearted moment in which they shared a muffled laugh.

As her mother stood and walked toward the door to exit Frances' bedroom, she turned around. "Oh, also, I wanted to compliment you on including Dolly and Duke on your Christmas list." Mrs. Dodge Wilson's eyes danced with amusement. "I'll see you at dinner at 6 o'clock." She softly closed the door as she exited Frances' bedroom.

Of course she had included her horses on her list. Frances loved her horses. She loved riding. Someday she would be a famous horsewoman![7]

On her way to the dining room, Frances knocked on Nanny Mary's bedroom door. "Come in." her nanny responded in a rather flat tone.

Frances opened the door to see her beloved nanny sitting oddly upright and rigid in her 'reading chair'. Mary often read before dinner and before bedtime. She loved romance novels best.

Frances had purchased her "Gentlemen Prefer Blondes' for the official first party in her Hilltop Lodge. Mrs. Wilson wouldn't permit Frances to sleep alone in her new playhouse… and suggested that Frances secure her nanny's agreement to spend the night. Mary had quickly agreed to the plan. Mary was always so agreeable—so cheerful.

---

[7] Frances Dodge was regarded as a true pioneer for women in the harness and saddle horse world. Her horse Wing Commander—that hailed from the famed Dodge Stables—was a legend in the saddle bred horse world.

But at this moment she looked lonely and sad. Nanny Mary was sitting in her favorite chair—a solitary figure with no book in her hands. She was not engrossed in a romance novel as Frances had expected to observe. Rather—she appeared to be staring intently at her bedroom closet door.

"Hello, Frances. I hope that your lessons went well today." She now turned her head and looked directly at Frances. "I know that it's not quite dinner time, but I have already placed your nightgown and fresh towels in your bathroom. I was thinking that I may go to bed a little early tonight."

Frances approached nearer to her. "Thank you. And… yes…my lessons were fine. But are you feeling well?"

A single tear fell down the left side of Nanny Mary's face. "I learned of some very bad news from my sister's husband today. He sent me a letter."

Frances now noticed the opened envelope and single sheet of stationary discarded on the lamp table. Frances wasn't certain what she should do—or ask. But then Mary continued.

"They lost the baby." she said.

Now Frances was confused. She stumbled over her words. "They can't find their baby?"

"I'm sorry, Frances. I should have been clearer. The baby was born too early. He was due in early March. The baby was too small. He died." Another tear fell.

Her final words saddened Frances. She was all too familiar with the untimely death of a family member. She could only think to say, "I'm sorry."

Mary then smiled. "Thank you, Frances. Frank, her husband, has assured me that they are hoping for another baby in the near future." This assurance seemed to sooth Nanny Mary's pain. She now focused on Frances. "But I haven't asked you what you needed from me."

"Well…I wanted to ask you something about Christmas… but we can talk tomorrow—or another day."

Mary reassured her that it was quite alright to continue the conversation. She even added some of her special brand of humor to their talk. "Did you want to hide something for Danny here in my room? I know that he may be planning a gift hunt—so I would advise you to stay one step ahead of him."

"You understand my brother quite well—and I appreciate your suggestion." Frances grinned as she reflected on her brother's mischievous nature. "But I wanted to ask if you would suggest a novel that I might give you as a Christmas present." Frances was pleased that the discussion of Christmas seemed to lighten her nanny's mood.

When Nanny Mary began to protest about receiving a gift—Frances remained firm on learning a book title. Mary thought for a minute—and then responded, "Oh, yes…there is a book I would like. As you know…I usually select romance novels. But I've heard so much about a new mystery writer. Her name is Agatha Christie.[8] Well…actually…I understand that this is her fifth novel. But it has received such great reviews. I would like to read this book." She declared with genuine interest and eagerness.

"What is the name of the book?" Frances asked. She did her best to stifle a giggle. Nanny Mary often seemed to omit important details when she was excited about something. But it was this enthusiasm that was so endearing.

---

[8] Agatha Christie was an English writer of novels, short stories, plays and poetry. Her novels included autobiographical books, romance works, and crime mysteries—but she is best known for the latter. Born in 1890, she became the best-selling fiction author of all time. She died in 1976.

"Oh—of course. It is called The Secret of Chimneys." Mary responded.

Frances continued down to the dining room—but first stopped in the kitchen to say hello to Hannah—and engage in some brief conversation. She was not only a great cook, but had a knack for making Frances laugh.

"Well, hello there my princess!" Hannah often referred to Frances as a princess. Over the years, she had grown quite fond of this pet name. "Have you visited your castle today?" Since Frances received her very special playhouse nearly one month ago—Hannah teased her by referring to Hilltop as a castle.

"Unfortunately—no." Frances sighed with exaggeration. "But I am hoping to make an appearance following dinner." Frances also liked to tease Hannah. "Would you be interested in joining me?"

Hannah chuckled. "Oh, no. Not tonight. I have plans."

"Hmm. Will you be writing, or reading, or knitting?" Frances was attempting to glean certain information from Hannah—information that might be of help in selecting the perfect surprise Christmas present. Since her mother had only approved her purchasing gifts for her tutor and her nanny—Frances would need to be very clever in selecting—and secretly giving—her gifts to the other house staff. It just wasn't possible to ask them directly about their wishes.

Hannah snorted, "No. None of those things interest me very much. My hobby is sleeping. Love it."

Frances laughed at such nonsense. But she also believed that she had learned something that might be useful. Sleeping. A gift related to sleeping…hmm.

At 7 o'clock the family finished dinner. It was dark outside…as the sun sets rather early in Michigan in the winter months. As her mother, stepfather, and brother began to amble toward the stairs to retire to their bedrooms for the evening, Frances cleared her throat and announced, "I would like to make a quick check on my Hilltop Lodge."

Mrs. Dodge looked skeptical. She asked, "Couldn't you wait until morning?"

"Mother…I promise to return within 25 minutes. I love to visit Hilltop each day…and earlier I was just too busy with my lessons and homework." Frances emphasized the words 'lessons' and 'homework'. She knew that her mother was a strong advocate for education, and thus this response would likely be viewed with great favor. Mrs. Dodge approached Frances.

"Well, alright. But please dress warmly." Mrs. Dodge kissed her daughter on top of her head and returned to the stairs.

Frances quickly changed into her boots and secured her coat, hat, and gloves. As she stepped out into the night air, the cold immediately greeted her—but it didn't bother her—she had successfully bargained the opportunity to visit her very special Hilltop!

It was perhaps a five minute walk to the wooded area where she ascended the hill to her extraordinary 'hideaway'. The snow wasn't deep yet—so it wasn't too difficult of a climb. Frances had the key in her coat pocket. She kept a second key in her bedroom in the middle desk drawer. She had considered giving this extra key to Patrick, but worried that her mother may somehow discover it was missing.

Patrick had only been hired a week ago to assist Hank in the stables—although he had actually been living at Meadow

Brook Farm in an abandoned work shed for about a month. In early November, Patrick had been walking from his family's farm in Milford to Detroit to find work—a distance of 25 miles—when he became ill and took refuge in the shed. Hank had found him—and took pity on him. He talked to Frances' stepfather—asking if they might hire the boy to help with the horses. Mr. Wilson trusted Hank's judgement—and agreed to the plan. Mr. and Mrs. Wilson did not know that Frances had been leaving 'treats' for Patrick in her Hilltop Lodge—or that he had brought her a birthday present on the evening of her overnight party with her nanny—before Mary had arrived. Frances and Patrick thought it best to keep their friendship a secret.

Frances stood before the beautiful entry door of Hilltop. The exterior lights of Hilltop were blazing—but the interior was black. As Frances opened the front door, she quickly turned on the living room light switch. Next she headed into the kitchen turning on that light. Finally, she headed for her guest bedroom and again lighted the room. She wanted to make it obvious that Hilltop was open for visitors.

Within a matter of minutes, there was a gentle tap at the front door. Yes…that would be Patrick! She rushed to open the door and greet him.

"Good evening, young lady." Patrick bowed slightly.

Frances found his characteristic bow to be endearing. She couldn't mask her amusement—her delight—at his appearance that night. Laughing…Frances responded, "I have two questions that I need to ask you…and then I must hurry back to the farmhouse."

"What important information might I provide you on this fine first evening of December?" He strode to the sofa and sat down—but still asked, "And would it perhaps be advisable that I sit on your sofa for this questioning?" Patrick's green eyes flickered with glee in teasing Frances.

"Yes. Please sit." Frances sat opposite him in a thickly upholstered wing chair. "Now…I was hoping that you could help me in deciding on a surprise Christmas present for Hank. He is so helpful to me with my horses."

Patrick leaned toward Frances and whispered, "I'm not certain if I could be of help to you. Does this really need to be a surprise—or could you ask him directly what he might like?"

Frances hesitated—and then whispered, "Not only does this need to be a surprise but it must also be a secret present."

Patrick now leaned back into the sofa. He no longer whispered. "Why must it be a secret?"

"Because my mother feels that it will be confusing to the staff if I purchase individual gifts for them. She and stepfather will be giving a bonus cash gift to each staff member."

At the mention of cash gifts, Patrick again leaned toward Frances. "Would that include me? he asked.

"I don't know." Frances suddenly felt uncomfortable discussing the topic of money with Patrick. He had only been hired a week back. She had no idea how her mother and stepfather would handle this type of staff situation.

Patrick sensed her change in mood. "I apologize for such a direct question." His easy smile returned. "So—you need to obtain something small—something that would not raise any suspicions as to the identity of the giver. And I suppose that I am to play the part of courier?"

"Yes!" Frances exclaimed. "I need you."

There was an awkward moment of silence. Those final three words expressed an essential truth. Since her father's death when she was just five years of age and her sister's death one year later, Frances often felt alone. She was taught by private tutors. Her family resided on a 1,500-acre farm far from the city. She had no friends. Fortunately, she had a natural talent when it came to horses. And Frances loved her two equine 'friends' Duke and Dolly. But Patrick brought a renewed sense of hope into her life. He caused her to laugh. And that was important.

Although sitting—Patrick again bowed. "And thus I am here to help you."

He suggested that she bake him a small chocolate cake. Patrick knew that Frances enjoyed baking in her Hilltop kitchen. And he knew that Hank enjoyed chocolate. So it was decided that she would make the cake very early on the morning of Christmas Eve day—that Patrick would come to Hilltop at approximately 7 a.m.—and that he would take the cake and deliver it to the small office in the horse barn and place on Hank's desk before he began his work day. No tags—no names. The timing should work.

Patrick remained seated as he asked, "And what might be your second question?"

Frances hoped that her expression wasn't as awkward and uneasy as she felt. Attempting to project a lighthearted air—she cheerfully inquired, "What gift might you like to receive at Christmas? I have your name on my list with nothing next to it."

Patrick responded quickly. "Frances...you interceded with Hank so that I might be employed here at Meadow Brook Farms. I now have three square meals a day, a roof over my head, and a bed to sleep in at night. How could I need more?" He stood and began to stride toward the front door.

Frances then stood. "But you might want more." She emphasized the verb 'want'.

He turned to face her. "No. I have your friendship. There is nothing else that I want."

And with those words, he went out into the cold night December air. Frances was not disheartened. She would surprise him. She left him thinking that she would drop the gift idea.

Chapter 2

Holiday Shopping

Thursday, December 2, 1926

Frances had been pestering her mother since Thanksgiving about a holiday shopping trip to Detroit—until finally last night during dinner—Mrs. Dodge Wilson agreed to take Frances Christmas shopping the very next day! Her mother had thought that it might be a bit early—but when looking over the family's December calendar—she conceded that a Tuesday or Thursday would work best since Frances did not have her lessons on those days—and all December Saturdays were filled. (Stores, of course, were not open on Sundays.)

Saturday the 4th was a prearranged lengthy meeting with the Meadow Brook Hall construction manager and the lead architect to update Mr. and Mrs. Wilson on their progress, and to seek guidance on some additional design decisions. Saturday the 11th was scheduled for Mr. Dodge's birthday luncheon at the new Savory Hotel in Detroit. (Mrs. Dodge Wilson had decided on this locale as opposed to the Jacoby's German Biergarten restaurant.) And the next weekend, on Saturday the 18th—the family would be attending Anna Dodge's Christmas party at her Rose Terrace mansion in Grosse Pointe. Frances loved visiting her aunt and thus was looking forward to this trip. And, of course, the next Saturday was Christmas Day!

Frances had finished her breakfast, but waited patiently at the dining table while the other family members ate. Following breakfast, she and her mother (and their driver John) would exit the farm and venture to Detroit. She was so excited for this holiday journey.

"Mother...I believe that I could complete my shopping in only two to three hours!" Frances declared. "I have rewritten my Christmas gift list and organized the items according to store department—books, toys, men's clothing—thus we can breeze through Hudson's!"

Mrs. Dodge Wilson smiled at her very mature 12-year-old daughter. "That is good to hear, Frances. But we'll also need to have John drive us to Sander's. We mustn't forget the chocolates."

"That would be appalling, reprehensible, shameful..." Frances shook her head back and forth in an exaggerated manner. She searched for another adjective. "Shocking."

Following breakfast, Frances and her mother departed Meadow Brook Farm with their driver John. They sat quite comfortably in the rear seat of the family's new 1926 Dodge Touring automobile. Frances loved to sit in a Dodge car. She was very proud of her father's business accomplishments. In the car, Frances and her mother chatted about many things. Finally, she introduced a topic of discussion that she had been avoiding.

"Mother...I will need a few minutes to shop on my own. I have money that I have saved...so it will be okay."

"But why?" Mrs. Dodge Wilson asked. "I know everything on your list."

Frances experienced a sudden surge of guilt. Her mother was not aware of her 'secret' list. She tried to think quickly of a reason for needing to shop alone. She sputtered, "There is something that I want to look for—for you."

"But I asked for you to write me a story." Her mother looked skeptical.

Frances nodded. "Oh, yes, I do plan to write you a story. But there is something else I want to look at."

"Well, okay." Her mother smiled patiently. "Let's plan to shop together from 10 a.m. until noon. We'll then have a quick 30-minute lunch. You can exit to begin your shopping—I'll stay behind and enjoy some tea. I may also shop a bit extra—and then we can meet at the front at 1 o'clock."

Promptly at 10 a.m., Frances and her mother passed through the main entrance of the J. L. Hudson's building. This was Frances' second visit to the newly built twenty-five story department store. She was just as amazed as the first time she visited. The store occupied an entire city block! (The 1881 structure had been demolished in 1923 and rebuilt in 1924.)

Her mother was a loyal customer. A key factor for this loyalty was Hudson's commitment to the Detroit community. Joseph L. Hudson served on many charities and civic boards (as did Mrs. Dodge Wilson). Hudson's was the first major department store in the country to stage a Thanksgiving Day parade for the citizens of its community—a full two years before Macy's in New York did so.

Frances and her mother navigated through the store using Frances' Christmas List as their guide. Frances was able to locate every item on her list for her stepfather (=a book about agriculture/farming, lined winter gloves, and a winter scarf), brother (=Lincoln logs and Tinkertoys), and Meadow Brook staff Miss Taylor and Nanny Mary (=the book Oh So Big by Edna Farber and the book The Secret of Chimneys by Agatha Christie respectively). Mrs. Dodge Wilson had approved Frances selecting the final gift items for Frances' tutor and nanny. Frances still wished to secretly select something small for the other staff (Anne, Hannah, Hank, John and George)—but that might not be possible today.

Since Frances only had half an hour to shop alone—she decided to concentrate on just one person from her secret list—Patrick. There were two items that she wanted to purchase. The first item was leather gloves. The Michigan winter weather had crept into their lives—slowly growing colder since mid-October. He worked outside so much of the day—thus he really needed a good pair of gloves. The ones that she spotted him wearing were thin with holes beginning to appear. It was probably a pair that was used as a back-up by Hank that he loaned to Patrick. The second item was more personal. Frances wanted to give him a new silver chain to hold the medals that he had shown her when he gave her the St. Anne medal—who he informed her was the patron saint of horses—for her birthday last month. Frances treasured this gift. She always kept the medal on her—usually in a pocket. She was afraid that if she wore the medal on a chain—her mother might notice it.

She was certain that she had enough money to purchase both gifts. When Frances and her mother parted following their lunch, Frances returned to the Men's Department first and again located the outerwear area where earlier she had selected gloves for her stepfather. The same floor clerk approached her and asked if he could be of any assistance. He didn't question why she had returned. Frances described the desired gloves, and he quickly led her to a counter. He lifted a pair of tan suede gloves with turn-back cuffs. "These are quite fashionable for gentlemen."

Frances hesitated. "Yes—these are quite nice. But my stepfather will be using these in our barn caring for horses."

The clerk looked confused...but then recovered quickly saying, "Of course. We also carry a line of premium work gloves."

Frances chose the thickest pair. She paid the clerk $1.79 for the gloves—thanked him—and headed for the elevator. The operator—a thin older black gentleman with an easy smile—asked where she wanted to go. "Jewelry, please."

Most of the counters were for women, but Frances successfully located the men's jewelry booth. It was dominated by watches. There were some rings, too—but she didn't see any chains. When the clerk asked how he might help her, she explained that she had a friend who carried religious medals in his pocket—and that she wished to purchase a chain for him to wear these medals around his neck.

"I'm sorry miss, but we don't carry chain necklaces for gentlemen." The clerk appeared to be a bit flustered. "Perhaps he might be able to use one of our keychains to hold the medals?"

Frances' disappointment was obvious. Fortunately, a clerk from a nearby women's booth overheard the conversation. He signaled for Frances to approach his station. Without hesitation, he shared an idea with Frances.

"While it's true that most of the necklace chains here in the women's area are very delicate—and thus wouldn't work well for your intended purpose—I do have one silver chain that is much, much heavier. It is a mariner link. Let me show you."

Frances' spirits lifted as the clerk placed the chain on a blue velvet display board for her to view. It looked perfect! "Yes, I think that this would be fine."

The clerk placed the chain necklace in a small black box lined with black velvet. Frances paid the man the sizable amount of $20.00 and then placed the box deep into her coat pocket. It was well hidden. Now there was just one more item to shop for!

Frances made a quick return to the book section. She asked the clerk if they had anything about European architecture or castles. She purchased a recommended book that contained numerous full-page photographs. This would be a perfect surprise for her mother.

Frances arrived just a few minutes late at their designated meeting place, but her mother did not appear agitated. John had just pulled the car in front of the massive doorway. He assisted them with loading their packages. Their next—and final stop—was Sander's chocolates. Mrs. Dodge Wilson allowed Frances to enter the store alone—so that whatever chocolates she selected for the family—including her Aunt Anna and new husband—would be a surprise. Her mother handed her a crisp twenty dollar bill—which not only covered the cost of chocolates for her mother, stepfather, brother, aunt and uncle—but Frances was also able to purchase small bags of candy for the other Meadow Brook staff that she wished to give a gift but her mother had not approved. She would need to be clever about this.

On the drive home, Frances and her mother again chattered about many topics—but the construction of the family's massive mansion dominated the conversation. Her mother was joyfully anticipating the meeting on Saturday morning with the distinguished architectural team.

"Oh, Frances. Meadow Brook Hall will indeed be a masterpiece!" Mrs. Dodge Wilson exclaimed.

Frances was in awe of her mother's boundless energy and enthusiasm. She was so passionate about Meadow Brook Hall. And, indeed, Mrs. Dodge Wilson would play the key role in the decision-making for this expansive home that years later would be called 'America's castle'.

"Your stepfather and I toured so many castle and manor houses when we honeymooned in Europe. I took extensive notes." These thoughts reminded Mrs. Dodge Wilson of an upcoming 'opportunity'.

"I meant to mention to you that for your stepfather's birthday luncheon I have made reservations at the new Savoy Hotel." she announced. And then added, "I loved your idea about the German Biergarten, but I am so anxious to see the interior of the new Savoy."

Frances asked, "Why is that Mother?"

"Well—it is an Italian Renaissance architectural design—and it was conceived and planned by Mr. Paul Kamper."[9] Mrs. Dodge Wilson said with great satisfaction.

Frances blushed just a bit when she asked, "Who is he?"

"He is the son of Mr. Louis Kamper...a renowned classical architect. Father and son have collaborated on a number of local buildings. We had considered hiring them for Meadow Brook Hall, but I was so pleased with the plans that Mr. William Kapp had shown me. He is with the Smith, Hinchman & Grylls firm of Detroit." Mrs. Dodge Wilson stopped only momentarily to catch her breath and then continued. "They have designed so many exquisite structures including the Detroit Opera House, the Hilberry Theater, the Detroit University Club and the Music Hall Center for the Performing Arts. And this past year, Mr. Kapp led the design team for the Florentine Renaissance Players Club on East Jefferson Avenue."

---

[9] The New York Times reported on September 4, 1930 that Mr. Paul Kamper had committed suicide after the failure of the Detroit Hotel that he built and owned. It represented a half-million dollar loss (=approximately eight million dollars today).

Frances loved to watch her mother engrossed in a discussion of architecture. She was exceedingly knowledgeable about this area—whereas Frances' passion was with horses. Thus Frances wasn't aware of the architectural 'prizes' to be found in Detroit. She would, however, learn from her mother.

"So now I know who Mr. Paul Kamper is…but I must confess that I've never heard of the Savoy Hotel….just the Book Cadillac Hotel."

"That's understandable. The Savoy just opened 10 weeks ago…on September 15th." Mrs. Dodge Wilson continued. "Actually…it is not yet completed. Only three of the twelve floors are open. It is on the corner of Woodward Avenue and Adelaide Street. The next time we travel to downtown Detroit together I will have John stop there!"

Frances beamed. "Thank you. I would like that."

"Oh—and Louis Kamper was the architect for the Book Cadillac." Mrs. Dodge Wilson added. "At 33 floors, it is the tallest building in Detroit, and the tallest hotel in the world."

"But the architectural firm for Meadow Brook Hall have designed many of Detroit's most beautiful buildings—right?" Frances asked.

Her mother smiled. "Yes. And I forgot to mention—you have just exited one of their stunning successes!"

Frances was puzzled. "What do you mean?"

"The Smith, Hinchman & Grylls firm constructed the twenty-five story J.L. Hudson's Department Store!"

They arrived home to Meadow Brook Farm a little past three in the afternoon. After carefully hiding her purchased gifts in her bedroom (Frances had two very special spots!) she changed into her riding clothes. She would have just enough time to ride—and visit Patrick at the stables—before preparing for the family's six o'clock dinner. After dinner she needed to finish some class work for tomorrow (Friday was a school day!). Then off to bed!

When she arrived at the stables, Patrick eagerly greeted her. "Hello!" He then confessed, "I thought that you would be riding this morning. I was disappointed when you didn't show."

"I couldn't." she responded. "My mother and I had a shopping trip planned in Detroit."

Patrick grinned. "Well, I missed you. Hopefully your shopping excursion was entertaining."

"Well, I'm not sure that I would judge it to be entertaining, but it was successful." Frances explained. "I was able to finish my Christmas shopping in just a matter of hours."

He didn't ask for any details about what items she purchased—and for whom. Frances wanted to surprise Patrick with her gifts—and she didn't want him to know ahead of time that she was giving him something in addition to the Sander's candy gift that she was giving to other staff. She knew that he had very little money, and she didn't want him to feel anxious or compelled to buy her anything.

"Ride with me." Frances suggested. "It's getting late and I don't want to be alone. It will be dark soon." It was true that sunset time in Michigan in early December was 5 o'clock—but Frances' real motivation was that she enjoyed Patrick's company. And he was a good rider who had a genuine knack with horses.

He bowed slightly. "Of course, Princess." Frances found his use of this pet name to be amusing. She wondered if he was aware that this was the pet name that Hannah the cook also favored.

"I'll saddle Dolly if you saddle Spirit." she offered.

Within a few minutes they were off to enjoy the 1,500 acres of Meadow Brook Farm. It was beautiful. Frances loved the feel of a horse—the pounding of their hoofs—the wind in her hair—the freedom of exploring. When they stopped to watch a herd of deer prancing across an open field, Frances suggested that they end their ride by taking a brief look at the construction site. As they approached the site—Patrick abruptly stopped his horse. This was his first time to view the future Meadow Brook Hall beginnings.

"My God, Frances." Patrick looked with amazement at the scope of the foundation. He was both astonished and bewildered at its size. "How large will your home be?"

Frances knew very well the approximate size. Her mother shared this information with her on multiple occasions. But she only responded, "Large."

Patrick brought his horse side-by-side to her horse. He looked intently at Frances. "Large?" His tone took on a somewhat sarcastic flavor. He waited patiently for her answer.

"Well…one of the wings will be just for house staff. And my mother wants there to be bedrooms available for guests."

She paused. "And she wants a large library. And a music room."

Frances found it difficult to meet his stare. She never really understood the wealth that her family possessed. And she certainly didn't understood the poverty that other families endured until Patrick entered her protected circle. She was just beginning to grasp an understanding of his situation.

Meadow Brook Hall would boast 110 rooms, fourteen fireplaces, twenty-six bedrooms (each with a built-in safe), elaborately carved wood and stone, handmade hardware and ceramic art tiles, intricately molded and carved plaster ceilings, ornately carved beams, gargoyles, hidden stairways, stained glass window insets, crystal and art glass lighting fixtures, gold-plated bathroom fittings—and more. In total, Meadow Brook Hall would comprise 88,000 square feet.

"Frances, how large will your home be?" Patrick repeated his question with an exaggerated slowness.

She met his stare. She answered nervously, "Eighty-eight thousand square feet."

Patrick moved his horse slowly forward. His head was down. Frances couldn't see his expression. He was mumbling something, but his words were incoherent.

"Patrick?" she began to move her horse forward—but stayed behind his steed. "I can't understand you."

He then turned his horse around so that he was facing Frances. He raised his head. "I said that this is unbelievable. Unreal." His voice was fairly even, but she thought that there was perhaps a trace or hint of anger in his undertone.

"I don't know how to respond to that." Frances then added, "I had no say or no part in deciding the size—so please don't be angry with me."

Perhaps it was her misreading of his response…her genuine expression of exasperation…her pleading tone of voice…but he found her absolute dismissal of involvement or 'guilt' to be hilarious. He began laughing—which caused Frances to feel puzzled—worried.

"What are you laughing at?" she asked.

Patrick attempted to regain control…to offer her an explanation… but when he experienced what his sister called 'one of his laughing fits' it was challenging. It wasn't easy to speak when one had trouble catching his breath. Frances signaled her horse to gallop.

"Wait." he cried out to her. "I'm sorry." He followed her gallop.

As they neared the stables, Frances slowed down—which allowed Patrick to catch up to her. He repeated, "I'm sorry." And then he added, "Please don't be angry with me."

Perhaps it was his misreading of her response…his panicked expression…his pleading tone of voice…but she found his feeble expression of apology to be hilarious. She began laughing—and he joined her in this laughter. It was an unbridled release of both apprehension and relief. The tension between the two disappeared. Due to the lateness of the hour, Patrick insisted on taking care of both horses, and Frances darted off to the farmhouse to prepare for family dinner.

Following dinner, Frances sat at her desk in her bedroom and completed her school work for tomorrow. She then took a warm bath and changed into her night clothes. As she laid in her bed, she again thought about her preparations for Christmas. It pleased her that she was able to finish her shopping—including those individuals on her 'secret list'. She just needed to wrap her family's presents, and the books for her nanny and tutor. Oh…she also needed to devise a plan to give the special Sander's candy—undetected—to the other staff—as well as a small chocolate cake to Hank. Patrick had suggested it. And, of course, there were Patrick's gifts. Should she also wrap these items? When he gave her the St. Anne medal for her birthday, he had used old newspaper and string to wrap her present. And she was thrilled. Perhaps fancy Christmas paper wasn't needed. She would think about that tomorrow. She was growing very, very tired. Sleep would come easy tonight—or so she thought. In the early morning, she awakened in a bit of a panic.

Chapter 3

Decorating Hilltop

Friday, December 3, 1926

Morning

Frances tapped lightly on her mother's bedroom door. It was 6 a.m. Breakfast would not be served for another two hours. But Frances was anxious to speak with her mother. She had awakened from a very vivid dream in which her Hilltop Lodge was beautifully decorated for the holidays. There was a splendid Christmas tree next to her fireplace. Beneath its bedecked limbs she found a present wrapped in plain brown paper and tied with string. In small print, she read, "To Frances. From Patrick."

The bedroom door opened. "Frances! Good morning. Is everything alright?" Mrs. Dodge Wilson had quickly draped a dark blue silk robe around her. She looked a bit puzzled—and concerned—due to the early hour.

"I'm sorry, Mother. Everything is fine. I just wanted to speak with you before breakfast." Frances suddenly felt sheepish. She wished that she had waited to approach her mother. She fixed her eyes on the floor—hesitant to say more.

Her mother smiled. "Of course. Let me finish dressing and I'll meet you downstairs in the front parlor."

Approximately 15 minutes had passed. Frances fidgeted in her chair. When her mother appeared in the doorway, Frances sat up straight and folded her hands on her lap. She again focused her eyes on the floor.

Mrs. Dodge Wilson crossed the room, gently kissed Frances on the top of her head, and seated herself next to Frances in a matching overstuffed wingchair. "What did you wish to discuss?"

Frances hesitated. "Mother. First, I wish to apologize for knocking on your bedroom door so early. I should have waited until after breakfast. What I want to ask you is important to me, but it is not urgent."

"If it is important to you, Frances, then it is important to me." Her mother smiled patiently. "I am assuming that this has something to do with horses?"

It was quite natural for her mother to make this assumption. Frances certainly had a passion for horses. However, her mother was not aware of Frances' recent infatuation with a young man with whom she had quickly established a rather fervent bond of friendship. The dream that awakened her this morning had served to jolt her realization that she needed to plan a Christmas celebration with Patrick at her Hilltop Lodge! And such a celebration would require some seasonal decorations—including, of course, a Christmas tree! Frances doubted that the staff...neither house nor grounds... would have fully decorated trees. And she wanted Patrick to enjoy this Christmas tradition. She felt certain that he had never had this opportunity with his family based on their circumstances.

"Frances? Something to do with horses?" Her mother interrupted her thoughts when she repeated her question.

"No—this is not about horses." Frances raised her head and met her mother's eyes. She took a deep breath and proceeded. "I wanted your permission to add some Christmas decorations to Hilltop." Frances waited.

"What type of decorations?" her mother asked.

Frances shrugged her shoulders, but responded rather quickly. "I was hoping for a wreath on the front door, and a small Christmas tree next to my fireplace."

Mrs. Dodge Wilson cocked her head to one side. She appeared to be giving serious consideration to this request. "Yes, I think that a wreath would be very festive. But I'm not certain about a tree. We will be placing a 14-foot fir in this parlor for the entire family to enjoy. I have purchased a large number of special decorations that are simply beautiful."

"But I spend time each day at my Hilltop—including doing much of my school work assignments. And I would make the decorations for the tree." Frances stopped. Then she added, "Please, Mother."

"Well…I suppose so…if this is something that is important to you." Her mother then added, "In addition to fashioning a wreath from pine boughs, I'll ask John to cut an appropriate size tree for you…and to make a stand for it."

Frances leaned over and hugged her mother. "Thank you so much!"

"You are welcome, dear. Would five days prior to Christmas be sufficient?" Mrs. Dodge Wilson was concerned about the tree. She didn't wish for it to become too dried out. Frances agreed with this time plan. She ate her breakfast quickly and attended her morning instructions with her tutor, Miss Taylor. Classes were held in both the mornings and afternoons on Mondays, Wednesdays and Fridays. (This was the same schedule for her brother, Danny, but he had a male tutor who met with him in a separate area.) Frances wasn't really thrilled with 'school' but she knew that her mother placed a high value on education and so she feigned interest in the classes. She also very much liked Miss Taylor.

Afternoon

When Miss Taylor finished the afternoon instructions and was collecting her books and papers, Frances remained in her seat. Her tutor noticed and asked, "Did you wish for me to continue our lessons past the hour?" Her playful manner put Frances at ease.

"Oh, no. But I was hoping that you might be able to help me with a special art project of sorts."

This peaked Miss Taylor's interest—as she also taught art—but Mrs. Dodge Wilson only wished for Frances to receive formal instruction in what she termed 'serious' subject matter. Nonetheless Miss Taylor responded, "How might I help?"

Frances explained how she wanted to have a Christmas tree in her Hilltop Lodge—and that her mother had given permission for her to do so—but that she needed to make the decorations herself.

"So—what would you like me to do?" Miss Taylor again posed the question.

Frances had carefully rehearsed her request. "Would you consider having a portion of my afternoon classes the week of December 13th be devoted to a secret seasonal art project?"

"I'll do better than that!" Miss Taylor declared without hesitation. "We'll start on Monday! We really only have two weeks. You see—I have a two-week holiday beginning on December 20th through January 1st." She explained further. "I'll be visiting my family in Philadelphia."

Frances was so thrilled that her tutor would support her artistic efforts to decorate her Hilltop Christmas tree! "Thank you so, so much."

"You are welcome! Now—each of us should bring some suitable items. I have colored paper—and wallpaper scraps as well. I also have glitter—which adds a special seasonal touch!"

Frances pondered, then said, "I could probably bring scraps of fabric. Would that help?"

Miss Taylor assured her that this addition would be good. "I do have some fabric paints. I'll bring these, too."

Evening

Later in the evening—but not too late—Frances tapped lightly on Anne's door. The housekeeper appeared quickly and greeted Frances with genuine delight. "Good evening!"

"Good evening." Frances repeated her greeting. "I was wondering…since you do a lot of sewing and such…if you might have any scraps of material that I might use?"

Anne's curiosity was peaked. "Most likely…but what purpose do you have in mind?"

"I would like to make some decorations for a small Christmas tree that will be placed next to my fireplace in Hilltop Lodge. I want my first Christmas there to be special!" Frances beamed.

Anne invited Frances to accompany her into the 'housekeeping room' to do a search. Actually, it was more of a large walk-in closet…but Anne called it her housekeeping room. Frances followed Anne. There were cleaning supplies, notebooks, uniforms—and a sewing machine with assorted materials in stacks!

"Wonderful!" Frances was pleased with the varied assortment.

Anne smiled. "Take what you like. Do you also need scissors—and a needle and thread?"

"I guess so." Frances responded. She wasn't really certain what she might need, but was confident that Miss Taylor would know the answer.

She began to select the fabrics that seemed most Christmas-like. There were five shimmering red satin pieces, two red and green checkered cotton scraps, and an extra-large silver linen square. She also took four of the solid white cotton pieces—as these might be useful for applying paints.

"I also have some shiny sequins." Anne added. "Let me show you."

Frances was not really certain what sequins were—but she was certainly willing to examine these!

Anne opened a wooden cigar box to reveal an assortment of small, colorful round objects. These were flat and shiny—catching and reflecting the light in the room beautifully.

"These are so pretty!" Frances gasped. "But how would I use these?"

Anne placed a silver sequin on the palm of her hand. "You can see a small hole in the middle. That is there so that you can sew these onto fabric—but you could also glue these on paper or wood decorations for your Hilltop Christmas tree!"

"I love these!" Frances exclaimed. Could I please have a few of each color?"

Anne nodded her agreement. She stepped further back into her housekeeping room and found a small white box. She filled it with five to ten sequins of each color. "I'm giving you more of the silver, gold, red and green—as these are the best Christmas colors!"

"Oh—how about some ribbon?" Anne had spotted a box of ribbon pieces when she grabbed the empty box for the sequins. "I have extra!"

Frances was so appreciate of Anne's help. "Yes, please."

"Well I'm happy to help." Anne handed Frances the full box. "Your Hilltop Lodge deserves a spectacular first Christmas!"

"Thank you so much." Frances was eager now for Monday to arrive so that she could show Miss Taylor the fabric swatches, sequins and ribbons. Suddenly she was struck by a need to change some of her timing plans. To do so—she would need to make a second trip to her mother's bedroom today with a request. No—she would wait till morning.

Saturday, December 4, 1926

Again—Frances was tapping lightly on her mother's bedroom door. But today she waited until 7 a.m. (rather than repeating yesterday's 6 a.m. journey). Mrs. Dodge Wilson opened the door in just a matter of seconds—and she was fully dressed for the day.

"Frances!" she exclaimed. "Good morning!" Her mother walked toward the sitting area of her bedroom and invited Frances to sit. "What might I help you with today?"

Frances chose her words carefully. She didn't want to disclose the exact number of hours that Miss Taylor was allowing for the art work—but she needed to offer an explanation or rationale for her new request.

"Mother—regarding the date for my Hilltop Christmas tree—you had mentioned yesterday that John could place the tree in my Hilltop Lodge about five days before Christmas." Frances proceeded. "Do you think that John could possibly have it ready earlier—by Thursday, December 16th?

Her mother titled her head to her right side as she considered this request. This was a favored pose of Mrs. Dodge Wilson. "Why so early?" she asked.

Frances had prepared for this question. Her reasoning was that she wanted to have the tree ready for decorating by Friday the 17th—so that Miss Taylor could witness—even participate—in its anointment! After all—Miss Taylor was providing the time, skill and some of the materials to make it possible.

"Well—I was really hoping that following our class sessions on Friday the 17th—I could invite Miss Taylor to see the tree." Frances continued. "I know that this is her last day until after the New Year holiday."

Mrs. Dodge Wilson appreciated Frances' bond with her tutor. "Of course, dear. I'll speak to John later this morning." And then she added, "But no candles on the tree. Too dangerous."

"I promise." Frances responded. In the days that followed, her mother never questioned Frances about her progress in making ornaments—or what materials she was using—or any specifics—for which she was very grateful.

※

Sunday, December 5, 1926

Sunday was Frances' favorite day of the week. All Meadow Brook staff had the day off from work—and thus she always saw Patrick on Sundays. When her family returned from church in the late morning, Frances announced that she was going to eat her lunch in her Hilltop Lodge. This had become a routine for Frances over the past month. Her mother or stepfather never questioned her about this choice. They were pleased that she so loved her custom playhouse. Indeed—it was the best birthday present!

Frances packed an extra-large lunch into the small picnic basket that was her very own. She made her way to Hilltop, unlocked the door, and waited for Patrick to arrive. Their agreed upon time was noon. Within ten minutes, there was a knock at her front door. She skipped from the dining table to the entryway and opened the door.

"Happy Sunday!" she exclaimed. Frances wasn't certain why she first offered this greeting in mid-November, but Patrick found it amusing—so she repeated it each week.

He smiled broadly and made his way to the dining table—where the picnic basket beckoned him. "I'm especially hungry today!" Although Meadow Brook staff were provided three good meals each day—the food prepared for the Dodge-Wilson family was much more extravagant.

"I think that you will appreciate Hannah's recipe for baked chicken." Frances added, "And her gratin dauphinoise potatoes, green bean almodine, and buttery crescent rolls."

Patrick laughed. "Stop, please. Let us begin." He sat at the table.

Frances stepped into her kitchen area and gathered the silverware, china plates, crystal glasses and napkins. She arranged these on the table—and then took out a bottle of milk from the refrigerator. She poured two servings. Patrick watched her intently as she prepared the table for their Sunday luncheon feast. He waited patiently. When she finally sat in her chair, he cleared his throat and said grace.

Patrick was Catholic. Frances' family, who were Lutheran, also typically began meals with grace. But Patrick seemed more passionate in his speech. When he was hired at Meadow Brook, he shared with Frances his profound feelings of gratitude. He also told her that he felt very fortunate to have her for a friend. Frances also felt fortunate, but was too shy to express her feelings. She wondered if she should tell him now. She stared down at her plate. Leaning across the table, Patrick placed his right hand on top of her left hand.

"A penny for your thoughts." Patrick was watching Frances as she appeared to be lost in some serious thinking. "Do you want to share those thoughts with me?"

Frances quickly regained her composure. Pulling both hands up to her head—she pushed her hair behind her ears. She redirected her thoughts and calmly stated, "You may think that this is a bit early—but I wanted to invite you to join me in my first Christmas celebration here at Hilltop." She attempted to display a very casual, nonchalant bearing—one of self-control and poise that she learned from her mother.

"When are you planning this celebration?" Patrick asked as he leaned back into his chair. He appeared to be abandoning his line of questioning about Frances' obvious preoccupation with something other than Christmas—but his playful grin signaled that her efforts to display such composure were not fooling him.

Frances managed a weak smile. "In two weeks—Sunday, December 19th."

"And how should I prepare for this celebration?" He was stepping up his mischievous manner. "Is special dress required? Should I bring any food, flowers, or seasonal items? Perhaps practice singing select carols?"

Frances laughed nervously—shaking her head back and forth. She lifted her gaze from her plate to his eyes. "No, no, and no!" She stated emphatically. "All that is required is your presence!"

"So all you need is me?" Patrick's stare increased her uneasy feelings.

She shifted her focus back down to her plate. "Yes."

The remainder of their luncheon was filled with conversation about the weather, her horses, and—of course—the construction of Meadow Brook Hall. At one o'clock, Patrick returned to the stables and Frances to the farmhouse.

Monday, December 6, 1926
Morning

Miss Taylor began the morning by clarifying her plan to integrate art instruction into her regularly scheduled classes on English, World Literature, Writing (each class occupying approximately 50 minutes in the morning) Geography, History, and Mathematics (each class occupying approximately 50 minutes in the afternoon). She would designate the final hour of both the morning and afternoon sessions to the special Christmas project. This would be accomplished by reducing the instruction time from 50 to 30 minutes for each subject area. Frances quickly calculated that she would have a total of six hours this week and six hours next week to create her tree decorations. She hoped to make as many as 50 or 60 so that her Hilltop Christmas tree would look truly festive. Perhaps this was an ambitious goal, but Frances was determined to succeed.

Frances usually enjoyed the morning classes—as she found the subject areas more interesting. But today it was difficult to concentrate. She was eager to begin making her tree decorations. Finally—a few minutes before 11 a.m.—Miss Taylor announced that it was time to begin! She announced that each day they would use the first ten-to-fifteen minutes of this special morning hour to plan or discuss ideas, and use the remaining time in the morning and the full hour in the afternoon to make the ornaments.

First, each unveiled their 'treasures'. Miss Taylor—as promised—had brought colored paper, a collection of wallpaper scraps, fabric paints and glitter. But she also provided seasonal templates for tracing or drawing such objects as a snowman and a candy cane. Additionally, she had gathered an assortment of 'nature' items including pine cones and berries. Frances displayed her fabric samples as well as the sequins and ribbons. And she shared her desire to create 60 ornaments in total.

"Well...then I would suggest planning to make approximately 10 ornaments each of our six designated class days."

"Miss Taylor—instead could we plan to finish in just 5 days—Monday, Wednesday and Friday of this week, but only Monday and Wednesday of next week?" Frances was hoping that Miss Taylor would not ask why. She wanted to surprise her with the trip to Hilltop on that final Friday to decorate the tree.

"I'm certain that we could follow that schedule, but I'm curious." Her instructor continued. "Why not Friday of next week?"

Well...it wasn't going to be possible to surprise Miss Taylor—which was probably better—as Frances had difficulty in keeping secrets. Except, of course, the secret about her friendship with Patrick. She was extremely careful about that secret.

Frances beamed. "Because I want to invite you to visit Hilltop Lodge to help me decorate the tree on that last day!"

Miss Taylor was flattered. "But of course. I would be honored to assist you in preparing Hilltop Lodge for the holidays! We will complete the work in five sessions."

Over the next two weeks, Frances and Miss Taylor not only crafted a total of 60 hand-decorated ornaments, but they also managed to make beautiful garland strands to complete the splendor of the first Hilltop Christmas tree.

Sunday, December 12, 1926

The Sunday hideaway lunches were never really routine for Frances and Patrick. Rather—these were occasions or junctures that built upon one another in which a genuine bond of friendship developed. On this particular Sunday—when Frances reminded Patrick that it was only two weeks until their special Hilltop Christmas party—it triggered for him sad memories of the prior year's Christmas day. He shared these feelings with Frances. For a poor farm boy who had lost his mother at the age of five—whose father continued to drink whiskey to hide his pain—who was separated on-and-off from his brother and sister as the children were 'passed off' to different relative's homes—the holidays served only to remind him that he had no real family. Although he had spent last Christmas reunited with his brother and sister—they were alone—no adult in the home, no dinner, and certainly no decorations or gifts.

"I'm so sorry." Frances really did feel his pain. And she was sad for him. "I wish that things had gone differently for you."

Frances wasn't certain how to comfort him. She suspected that Patrick might believe that her life was problem free because her family possessed wealth—actually a great deal of money. But this was far from the truth. It would be painful for her to share this truth with him, but she decided to do so. As they sat side-by-side on her sofa in front of a roaring fire, she kept her gaze on the fireplace.

"You know that I also lost a parent—my father—when I was five years old. And then three years later, I lost my sister". Frances was trying so hard not to cry. She was afraid to look directly at Patrick as she shared some of her own sad history.

"What happened?" he asked.

Frances continued to watch the fire. "My father, John Dodge—as you know he established the Dodge Motor Company with his brother—had went to New York for an automobile show. He was exposed to the Spanish flu, then developed pneumonia—and died in his hotel room at the

Ritz-Carlton. Three years later my sister, Anna, died from complications from measles. She was just four years old."

Patrick whispered, "I am sorry." He then added, "And I wish that things had gone differently for you."

Frances now looked at Patrick. His eyes were glazed. She thought that he might cry, and she wasn't prepared for this. But instead he posed another question.

"Do you remember your last Christmas with your father?"

Frances responded quickly, "Yes, I do. It was just a week before he and his brother departed for their business trip to New York. They were very excited about attending the automobile show. He and my Uncle Horace were not only brothers and business partners, they were the best of friends." Frances stopped talking for just a few seconds, and then continued. "Uncle Horace died eleven months after my father – who died on January 14th. Some family members claimed that he died of a broken heart. He was like a second father to me…"

Patrick waited. When she said no more on the subject, he reflected, "I don't really remember the last Christmas with my mother. But I do remember some good times—of her playing with me, my brother and sister. But after her death, my family just split apart." He now kept his gaze on the fire in front of them.

Frances reached for his hand and held it. Neither of them said a word for the next ten minutes. And then Frances released her grip on his hand.

"I need to return home. My family will be expecting me." As soon as she said these words, she regretted it. She had a family. He lacked one.

But Patrick did not seemed bothered by her choice of words. He smiled and said, "Thank you for planning this party in two weeks."

Frances nodded.

Friday, December 17, 1926
Morning

At the end of their morning classes, Frances reminded Miss Taylor to meet her at 1 o'clock on the front porch of their farm house. There would be no afternoon classes today! They would be decorating her Hilltop Lodge Christmas tree! Frances had also arranged for some refreshments for her and Miss Taylor to enjoy. Her playhouse was quite elaborate—including the kitchen which had a working refrigerator and stove. In fact, Hilltop was the very first 'residence' in the Detroit metropolitan area to have electricity in each room!

Afternoon

The prior evening, Frances had carefully packed her newly made tree ornaments in a small suitcase. Following lunch, she retrieved the suitcase from her bedroom. She dressed warmly (a coat, hat, gloves and boots were certainly necessary in Michigan's late December weather). She remembered to take her Hilltop key with her—wedged securely in her right coat pocket. As she stepped onto the large wrap-around porch of the farmhouse, the crisp cool air greeted her. In the distance, she could hear the construction crew for the Meadow Brook Hall mansion. Although the anticipated completion date was two years away, Frances was nevertheless excited each time these sounds reached her.

Within seconds she was joined by Miss Taylor.

"Ready?" she asked.

"Ready!" Frances responded.

There was just a small amount of snow on the ground—and thus their walk to Hilltop was relatively easy. A festive pine wreath on the front door greeted their arrival at the playhouse. When Frances unlocked the door and stepped into the living room, she spied the nicely shaped pine tree standing at least six feet tall to the right of the fireplace. John had delivered it—and secured the tree in a stand—as promised.

Miss Taylor noted the direction of Frances' gaze. "It is a beautifully shaped tree!" she said.

"Thank you! I'll be sure to tell John." Frances was pleased with his choice.

"Before we begin—could you provide me a tour of your Hilltop Lodge?" Miss Taylor asked.

Frances responded with pride, "But of course!" Frances placed the suitcase on the dining table, and gave Miss Taylor an official house tour describing each room.

Miss Taylor was amazed at the detail and beauty of Hilltop Lodge. The six-room playhouse was a gift to Frances from her mother and stepfather for the twelfth birthday. Other wealthy Detroit area families, including Edsel and Eleanor Ford, owners of the Ford Motor Company, would later present their daughters with elegant playhouses. But Frances was first! The same architectural firm that the Dodges hired to design Meadow Brook Hall were also hired to first build her playhouse. It was designed to resemble an English country house or cottage with a brick exterior and an interior with beautiful oak paneling and woodwork. There was a living room, kitchen, dining room, two bedrooms and a bathroom (with plumbing) as well as a basement. Mrs. Dodge Wilson had some very practical reasons for gifting Frances with such a playhouse that had the style of interior decoration and furnishings similar to those planned to grace Meadow Brook Hall. She felt that this small-scale of Meadow Brook Hall was the ideal place for Frances to practice housekeeping, child care, budgeting and entertaining. But for Frances, Hilltop Lodge was a protected space, a safe haven, a hideaway of sorts. And it was here that she met Patrick.

At the conclusion of the tour, Frances returned to the dining table and opened the suitcase to begin their 'work'. (It was really a labor of love!) Miss Taylor had advised that they first arrange the garland on the tree prior to attaching the single ornaments. Together they had successfully made a total of five fifteen-foot strips! Each band was fashioned with an assortment of popcorn, red berries, ribbons, and pinecones. As they carefully draped each of these bands on the tree limbs, Frances began to envision the beauty of her first Hilltop Christmas tree.

The next step was to attach the single ornaments. They began with the candy canes. They had used a template that Miss Taylor had provided to cut the classic curved canes out of heavy cardboard—to which they had glued cutout white fabric and then painted red stripes. The final step was the addition of glue and sprinkling of white and red glitter. There were a total of 20 candy canes. Frances spaced these with great precision on her tree—wanting to achieve equal spacing of these ornaments. Miss Taylor assisted by suggesting changes in the positioning—a little to the right—a little higher—and so on.

Following the candy canes, Frances selected the snowmen. Again, Miss Taylor had provided a template which was used to trace onto both heavy cardboard and the white fabric. Once cut—they glued the fabric on the cardboard and painted a black stovepipe hat as well as button eyes, mouth and nose. As a final touch, they used the red and green checkered fabric to cut a neck scarf for each of the 20 snowmen. It was a very festive touch. Again, Frances carefully spaced these on the tree—with Miss Taylor offering suggestions.

"How about a refreshment intermission?" Frances suggested.

Miss Taylor nodded her approval.

Frances took juice from her refrigerator and poured each of them a glass. She then removed a plate from her cupboard that displayed large sugar cookies in the shape of Santa Claus' face. Red and white icing had been used on his hat, coconut on his beard, and two raisins for the eyes.

"These are adorable!" As she took her first bite, Miss Taylor added, "And delicious! Did you make these?"

Frances blushed. "No. Our cook, Miss Hannah, deserves all of the credit."

The final set of 20 ornaments were Frances' favorites. Again a template was used—this time a star—but each one was individually decorated—thus each was unique. Either the red satin or the silver linen fabric was first glued on the cardboard star—but some had sequins, some had glitter, some had paint—or some combination. Each was beautiful. But one in particular—one with the greatest detail—was exceptionally stunning. If you were to look very, very closely—you could read 'To Patrick' in small cursive writing in the center. When this last ornament was hung, Frances stood back and observed with great joy—and pride—her first Hilltop Lodge Christmas tree. As she stood there, she realized that she was crying. But these were definitely tears of happiness. Miss Taylor had also observed the tears, but didn't wish to embarrass Frances by pointing it out.

Instead she exclaimed, "This is perhaps the most beautiful tree that I have ever helped to decorate!"

Frances responded, "Thank you for being here. Thank you for making this possible." And then she added, "I dedicate this tree to those who made it possible—including my tutor!"

"I was happy to help." Miss Taylor released a contented sigh.

As they exited her playhouse together, Frances was busily chatting with Miss Taylor about the Christmas party at Rose Terrace tomorrow night in Grosse Pointe. She had carefully constructed her shopping list. In her excitement, Frances forgot to lock the front door of her precious Hilltop Lodge.

Chapter 4

Visiting Rose Terrace

In 1912, two years before Frances' birth to Matilda and John Dodge, her Aunt Anna and Uncle Horace (John Dodge's brother who co-founded the Dodge Motor Company) had commissioned the famed architect Albert Kahn to construct an expansive red sandstone mansion on Jefferson Avenue in Grosse Pointe, Michigan. The house name or title of Rose Terrace, however, was not due to the red color stone but rather was the result of the vast collection of rose bushes that Anna Dodge had the landscape workers plant on both the upper and lower terraces of the mansion. Roses were Anna's favorite flower. A multitude of large windows provided a breathtaking view of Lake St. Clair as well as the massive, beautiful gardens positioned between the mansion and lake.

In 1920, the 'first' Rose Terrace was regarded as one of the finest homes in America. It had been important for Horace Dodge to provide his family with a home that reflected his wealth. He wanted his wife and children to enjoy the benefits of the fortune he and John Dodge had earned. Approximately six years following the death of Horace Dodge (1920), Anna Dodge remarried (1926). Her second husband, Hugh Dillman, was a former silent film actor. When they married in 1926, the out-of-work actor was 41 years of age—Anna Dodge was 55 years of age.[10] The 14-year-age difference was fodder for much gossip. Dillman moved into her mansion in Grosse Pointe—and soon was encouraging Anna to plan and build a 'second' more lavish Rose Terrace on a prime nine acre site also located on Lake St. Clair. Dillman urged Anna to enjoy her wealth. Anna subsequently hired Horace

---

[10] The first Hollywood sound or 'talkie' film, The Jazz Singer, opened in movie houses in 1927. It was highly successful. Soon after—sound films were the standard—and many silent film performers were unable to make the changeover or transition.v *en.wikipdeia.org*

Trumbauer to design the new mansion.[11] Anna also worked closely with Sir Joseph Duveen, a famous art dealer. Anna and Hugh toured Europe for more than two years collecting prized antiques and works of art for their home. The new Rose Terrace would open in 1934.[12]

---

[11] Trumbauer, a native of Philadelphia, was a prominent architect who was well known for designing mansions for America's most wealthy families. His first significant client was sugar magnate William Welsh Harrison. In1893, he designed Grey Towers Castle for him. Harrison subsequently recommended Trumbauer to an associate, Peter A. B. Widener, a highly successful real-estate developer. It was his Georgian-revival manor, Lynnewood Hall, that launched Trumbauer's career. Most of his work was done in Philadelphia, New York and Newport—but he accepted Anna Dodge's invitation to come to Detroit. *en.wikipdeia.org*

[12] In 1971, Rose Terrace was designated both a Michigan State Historic Site and was listed on the National Register of Historic Places. But this extraordinary home—referred to as an 'American Cultural Treasure' (David Netto, June 1, 2017) was demolished in July of 1976. Anna Dodge had lived in seclusion for many years. When she died in 1970, furnishings and artwork were either willed to the Detroit Institute of Arts or sold by Christie's. Upkeep of the expansive home was very costly thus there were no buyers. Some local groups worked to save the mansion due to its historical significance but these efforts failed. *en.wikipdeia.org*

But in December of 1926, Frances Dodge was thrilled to be visiting her Aunt Anna—and to meet her new husband of seven months Mr. Dillman—to experience what would surely be a splendid Christmas party in their mansion (the original Rose Terrace!). Frances had, of course, previously visited Rose Terrace many times when she was a young child. However, the number of visits decreased significantly following the death of her father and his brother. But she retained vivid memories of her father and uncle—chasing the children on the lawn. Laughing. Sharing stories. And on their final summer together—the two brothers attempting to drive one of their Dodge automobiles down to the lake—and across the manicured lawn. Aunt Anna was chasing behind the car and shouting at them to cease their high jinks while the other family members were laughing so hard that tears streaked their faces. John and Horace were known for their rambunctious antics or horseplay.

In addition to her fondness for her Aunt Anna, Frances was also excited to see some of the new features added to Rose Terrace. Since her own mother frequently engaged in lengthy conversations about the plans for Meadow Brook Hall, Frances wondered what similarities and differences there might be when comparing the two homes. She often dreamed what her bedroom in Meadow Brook Hall would look like. Her mother had assured her that she could select some of the design elements for her room. She was anxious to move into her new bedroom. Of course at that time, Frances didn't realize that it would take three years for the builders to complete such a massive project.[13]

Saturday, December 18, 1926
Morning

Following breakfast, Frances dressed for riding. Before heading for the stables, however, she decided to stop at Hilltop to once again view her beautiful Christmas tree. She also wanted to recheck her kitchen supplies to insure that she had everything in place for her special holiday celebration with

---

[13] The groundbreaking for Meadow Brook Hall was held on her mother's birthday on October 19, 1926. Meadow Brook Hall was completed in the summer of 1929 at a cost of nearly four million dollars. The housewarming party was held on November 19, 1929, just three weeks after the stock market crashed that started the Great Depression. And yet the party, attended by 850 guests, was lavish. *Book One Hilltop Lodge: Frances' Birthday Celebration*

Patrick on Sunday. Upon arriving, she stood momentarily at her front door to admire the wreath. As she removed the key from her coat pocket and proceeded to place it in the lock—the door eased a bit forward—and she then realized that the door was already unlocked. This knowledge sent a brief wave of concern through her. She pushed the door halfway open and shouted, "Is anyone in here?"

There was only silence. She knew that she had last exited Hilltop the previous day with Miss Taylor following the Christmas tree decoration and dedication. Perhaps in all of her excitement she had forgotten to lock the door? Her mother kept a second key to be used in an emergency—or if Frances misplaced her key. Since there had been no emergency, and Frances had not lost her key, she didn't believe that her mother would have opened the door. And she certainly would not have left it unlocked.

Frances stood in the entryway another two minutes—debating her course of action—but then decided to proceed with her plans. She walked first to the kitchen and determined that everything was ready. China, glassware, and Christmas-designed linen napkins on the table—and the food and drink she selected was in the refrigerator. She then entered the living room area and stood in front on the fireplace.

"It is truly beautiful!" she said aloud as she admired her and Miss Taylor's handiwork. Together they had crafted a handsome Christmas tree. But as her eyes moved from top to bottom of the tree, Frances suddenly jerked her head back to the top. She noticed something different in the decorations. Moving slowly forward, she stared in astonishment at a new 'addition' to her tree. Amid the handmade garland, candy canes, snowmen and stars—was a small painted horse. Its coloring resembled her own horse, Dolly. Frances was puzzled—and perhaps a little alarmed. Someone had entered her Hilltop Lodge.

Was the ornament placed there by Patrick? It appeared to be handmade—and she seriously doubted that it could be her mother's work. She concluded that it must have been Patrick who visited her Hilltop Lodge. No one else would make such an ornament. Her feelings were divided. She was disappointed because she wanted the decorated Christmas tree to be a surprise on Sunday. But she was also excited to think that Patrick may have made her such a personal gift. She carefully locked the front door--and headed for the stables.

When she arrived at the stables, Patrick had already saddled Dolly. "Hello! I've been waiting for you." He was in a good mood—very cheerful. Frances hated to threaten that mood, but she dove right into her burning question.

"Did you enter my Hilltop Lodge last night or early this morning?" Her gaze was intent—serious.

Patrick suddenly sensed that his new friend was perhaps upset. He was taken back by the directness of her question. He responded truthfully, "Yes, I did." And then added, "I had a surprise for you."

Frances sighed. "I love the horse ornament, but I wanted my decorated tree to be a surprise for you on Sunday."

"I'm sorry, Frances. My plan was to place the horse in your door wreath, but when I realized that the front door was unlocked, I decided that it might be better to place it on the tree." He moved a step closer to Frances. He whispered, "Will you forgive me?"

Frances found it impossible to stay angry at Patrick. "Yes. I suppose that it is really my fault. In my hurried excitement yesterday, I must have exited Hilltop without locking the door. But you must promise me to pretend to be surprised when you come over tomorrow afternoon."

"I have already erased last night from my memory." Patrick then changed the subject. "You'll be leaving for your Aunt's estate soon?"

Frances nodded. "Yes. Rose Terrace."

"Tell me a little about it." After learning some of the details of the plan for Meadow Brook Hall, Patrick was curious about the homes of the very rich.

Frances felt awkward. How does one describe such an extravagant home to someone who struggles so much for so little? Finally she responded, "I'm sure you will find it to be excessive. Over-the-top."

"Oh, please satisfy my curiosity." Patrick smiled widely. "I promise not to judge."

Frances complied. She described the setting on Lake St. Clair...the sculptured terraces that separated the mansion from the water. She defined the purposes of several key rooms including the music room, library, dining hall, and ball room. She referenced some of the prized art works—and furniture pieces. Patrick listened intently. He seemed to be absorbed in her narrative. When she announced that she needed to take her ride on Dolly—that lunch was soon and she would then need to ready herself for the trip to Rose Terrace—it was if she had broken a trance.

"Let me help you up." Patrick gave her a boost. "Enjoy your ride. I wish that I could join you today, but Hank has some pressing tasks for me."

Frances nodded her understanding of the situation. "Today will be a short ride. I should return in probably twenty to thirty minutes."

Afternoon/Evening

Following her ride, Frances had a quick lunch with her family. She then bathed and dressed for her Aunt's holiday party. Her mother had purchased her a very festive green satin dress. She felt beautiful in this holiday creation acquired from the Hudson's department store. Her brother, Danny, complained throughout lunch about being forced to wear a dress shirt, pants, jacket and tie. His tirade continued in the car until Mrs. Dodge Wilson reprimanded him. But he continued to sulk—quietly—his arms crossed defiantly over his suit coat—with impatient sighs escaping about every ten minutes. Frances was tolerant of her brother's pouting.

To be fair—it did take nearly an hour and a half to make the journey to Rose Terrace. It was approximately 30 miles between Meadow Brook Farm in Rochester Hills and Rose Terrace in Grosse Pointe Farms. The roads were fair, but certainly not perfect. John generally drove at an average speed of 25 miles an hour (although he could drive up to 40 miles an hour). But the wait didn't really bother Frances. She was excited to attend her Aunt Anna's Christmas party—and to be honest—she was even more excited thinking about her secret party with Patrick that was scheduled for tomorrow afternoon. So she enjoyed this opportunity to reflect.

They arrived promptly at 4 o'clock. Anna had planned for her guests to arrive early so that they could enjoy the view of the lake before dinner. (The sun would set by 5 o'clock!) Of course, the rose bushes were not in bloom in Michigan in December, but Lake St. Clair—especially at sunset—was still quite beautiful. And Anna had planned the perfect holiday party. There were a wide variety of delicious h'ordeuvres and specialty drinks—as well as a gifted piano player with a very talented vocalist who sang our favorite Christmas carols. During this time, there were also some gifts exchanged. Anna and Hugh loved the chocolates that Frances had selected for them. And Frances cherished the silver charm bracelet with a single charm—of course, it was a horse. The presents were followed by a truly magnificent six-course dinner on a candelabra decked table with numerous floral arrangements in red and white. This feast was followed by more entertainment including an orchestra band and dancing. The children were encouraged to join in the fun. At 9 o'clock, many of the guests were departing.

It had indeed been a splendid Christmas party! Her Aunt Anna seemed so contented. Frances had not seen her this happy since before the death of Uncle Horace. Regardless of stories about Hugh Dillman—that he only married Anna because of her immense wealth—Frances was glad that she had found Mr. Dillman. It seemed to Frances that he was the reason for her aunt's renewed energy and humor. She had found a fresh hope for tomorrow in this man.[14] Of course, the age difference between Anna and Hugh (again—he was 14

---

[14] It was reported that the marriage was already in trouble before the second Rose Terrace opened in 1934. There were rumors of his infidelity. However, Anna and Hugh did not divorce until 1947. Thus the marriage did last for twenty-one years (1926-1947). Anna did not marry again. She spent the remainder of her days secluded at Rose Terrace.

years younger than Anna) contributed to the unkind rumors. But Frances found her new Uncle Hugh to be a very nice man. He was charming and attentive. He laughed frequently. Anna needed that.

Late Evening

When the family returned home that evening—it was rather late. Thus they were understandably surprised when there was a knock at the front door of the farm house at 10:30 p.m. Each family member, with the exception of Mrs. Dodge Wilson who upon arrival had went quickly upstairs, were still removing their coats and boots in the farm house's foyer. Mr. Wilson opened the door to find Hank, who managed the stables at Meadow Brook Farm, standing on the porch looking anxious.

"I'm sorry for the late hour, Mr. Wilson. But I wanted to share some news with you about one of the horses." Hank looked at Frances apprehensively.

Mr. Wilson turned to the children. "Frances. Daniel. Please go to your bedrooms now." The tone of his voice was sympathetic—but strong.

Danny turned and began to climb the stairs, but Frances didn't move. "Is it Dolly or Duke?" Her voice trembled.

"No, Miss Frances. It is Spirit." Hank then turned to Mr. Wilson and continued. "He injured one of his back legs. I have treated and wrapped it, but wondered if you might stop by the stables in the morning?"

Mr. Wilson responded, "Of course I will."

Frances remained motionless. The two men now turned their attention to the young girl. Mr. Wilson was about to speak when she blurted out, "I want to see my horses."

Mr. Wilson gently placed his hands on her shoulders. "It is very late."

Frances pleaded with her stepfather. "Please let me go to the stables for just a few minutes."

"If you want, Mr. Wilson. I'd be happy to walk Frances back and forth." Hank volunteered to do this because he felt so bad for young Frances. He was aware of just how much she loved those horses.

Mr. Wilson studied her face. The fear was obvious—so he reluctantly agreed to Hank's offer. Now he would need to explain this decision to his wife. He began his ascent up the stairs.

When they arrived at the stables, Hank stayed outside while Frances hung her coat on one of the hooks by the stable door. She moved quickly to the back of the horse barn where the stalls for Dolly and Duke were located. And there stood Patrick. She almost ran into him—as she didn't expect anyone to be there.

"Frances. What are you doing here this time of night?" Patrick was concerned. "Is everything okay?"

She smiled weakly. "Hank told the family that one of the horses were injured. I just wanted to check on my Dolly and Duke."

Patrick smiled. "Your love for those horses never ceases to amaze me." He continued in a joking manner. "Ah...to be the object of such total affection and devotion."

Frances moved past him. "I just want to see Dolly and Duke...to stroke and nuzzle each of them... and to say goodnight."

Patrick was focused on Frances—and not the horses. "Might I also add that you look especially beautiful in that green dress. It's a very flattering color for you." Patrick then added, "Green is the Irish color, you know."

Frances was certain that she was blushing. She kept her head bent low as she petted each of her horses. Finally she stammered, "Thank you. My mother selected this dress for me to wear to Rose Terrace."

"I commend her choice." Patrick then bent down low so that he could be face-to-face with Frances. "Perhaps you could wear it to our luncheon party tomorrow afternoon?" His eyes twinkled with mischief.

Frances stood and crossed her arms in a somewhat defiant pose. "If I wore this dress tomorrow—in the middle of the day—my mother would be highly suspicious."

Patrick stood up. "So…she wouldn't approve of our friendship? Or our Christmas luncheon?" Patrick's tone had become just a bit more serious.

Frances didn't wish to hurt his feelings, but she wanted to be honest with him. "I don't think so." And then she added, "But I don't care. And besides—I think that I enjoy having a secret friend."

"Ah...so I am simply a diversion for you? An amusing pastime?" He did his best to appear distraught...forlorn. This was the type of behavior or performance that defined Patrick.

Frances played along. "Certainly. And please do your best to avoid becoming a bore. Once I grow weary of you—that will end the Sunday lunches." She started to walk past Patrick when he grasped her left hand and turned her toward him.

"Then I will do my absolute best to keep you amused." And as he bowed slightly—he kissed her hand—and released it.

Now Frances was one hundred percent convinced that she was blushing. Fortunately the barn was not well lit. She walked toward the entrance—perhaps a bit shakily--grabbed her coat off the hook—and exited. Hank was waiting for her about twenty-five feet from the entrance to the barn—leaning against a fence post.

"Ready, Princess?" he asked.

At first Frances was startled. She had actually forgotten about Hank. The chance meeting with Patrick had flustered her. She now realized that she may have spent too much time in the barn. Would Hank be suspicious?

Hank repeated his question. "Are you ready now?" He appeared normal...relaxed.

Frances nodded and they walked side-by-side up to the farm house.

"Thank you, Hank." she said. "I feel so much better now."

Hank responded, "You are welcome. He opened the front door for Frances—where her stepfather was waiting.

"I was worried." said Mr. Wilson. "Was everything okay?"

Frances responded first. "I'm sorry. I just wanted to spend a little time with Dolly and Duke."

Hank followed. "No problems, Mr. Wilson. The time just got away from us."

"I understand. Thank you for walking Frances." Mr. Wilson locked the front door after Hank stepped off the porch. He turned to his young stepdaughter and said, "Frances—it's eleven o'clock. Up to bed now." He bent over and kissed the top of her head. "Your mother was not too pleased with me for allowing you to visit the stables at this hour of night."

Frances felt fortunate to have such an understanding stepfather. "Thank you. I really do appreciate all that you do for me."

Once in bed, Frances found it difficult to sleep. Patrick's kiss on her hand had taken her totally by surprise. She was still in a state of shock—of disbelief. Had it really happened?

And yet, she was also happy. But also fearful. Frances was certain that her mother would not approve. And if she learned of this incident, she might discharge Patrick. He needed the job in the stables. It provided him a room, a bed, three meals a day and some spending money. Frances didn't think that Hank had witnessed the kiss. When she exited the stables, he was quite a distance away—just leaning against the fence and staring at the night sky. As these thoughts rolled over and over again in her head, Frances finally drifted to sleep.

Chapter 5

Holiday Luncheon

Sunday, December 19, 1926

Morning

For Patrick

Patrick was just finishing his morning tasks in the stables when Hank entered. Patrick immediately knew that something was wrong. Hank looked troubled.

"I need to speak with you—on a personal matter." Hank motioned for Patrick to join him in his small 'office'. This is where Hank had a desk of sorts and a wood filing cabinet. He kept records on the horses, feed, expenses, etc. There were two chairs.

"Patrick...you are a good worker. You ask the right questions. You learn quickly. You always finish any tasks that I give to you." Hank looked uncomfortable. He hesitated, then added, "But you need to understand about boundaries."

Patrick now looked even more uncomfortable than Hank. "Boundaries?" he asked—although he had a sinking feeling that he knew the answer to his question.

"I think you know what I'm talking about here." Hank replied. He then lowered his voice. "If you continue to see Frances—you could endanger your employment here at Meadow Brook Farm."

There was an awkward silence as Patrick tried to gather his thoughts. "We are just friends. No more." Patrick then added, "Frances asked her mother if it would be okay if I went riding with her sometimes. Especially when it nears night time. She said okay."

Hank sighed. He really did like Patrick. "I know that you meet on Sundays in her Hilltop Lodge. And I believe you when you describe this as a friendship. But her mother and stepfather may view it differently."

Patrick didn't really know how to respond to Hank's argument. He didn't realize that anyone else knew about their Sunday lunches. And in his heart—he knew that Hank was right about Mr. and Mrs. Wilson. Frances' parents would not approve of their friendship.

"I'm sorry, Hank. I promise you that today will be the final luncheon."

Hank asked, "Today?" He was curious.

Patrick explained further. "You see—she is so excited about having a Christmas party at Hilltop. I'll go, but I will explain the situation to her. She'll understand."

"Can I ask you something?" Hank waited for Patrick's response.

Patrick nodded. "Go ahead. Ask."

"Your lives are so very different. What do you talk about? What do you have in common?" Hank was genuinely perplexed. "I know that you each like horses—but other than that—I'm a bit mystified."

Patrick responded, "It's true that we share a common interest in horses. But I think that it is because of our differences that our friendship grew."

Hank still looked perplexed. So Patrick added, "We have one other thing in common. We each lost a parent at about the same age. And that experience changed us."

"Well...I would strongly urge you to end the Sunday lunches after today." Hank placed a hand on Patrick's shoulder. "Of course, you could continue to ride together."

Patrick thanked Hank and exited the stables. Now...how to tell this news to Frances.

For Frances

Sunday mornings were spent as a family at their place of worship. Both Frances' mother and her stepfather were quite involved in their Presbyterian Church—which was where Matilda Dodge had met fellow church member Alfred Wilson (who would, of course, become her second husband). Due to this extensive involvement—which included membership on various church committees—the Dodge-Wilson family often lagged behind following the conclusion of the regular Sunday morning service.[15]

And today, the church service seemed especially lengthy. Generally, Frances loved the December Sundays before

---

[15] Mrs. Dodge Wilson was particularly active in public service. She supported more than forty organizations with both her time and money. The Salvation Army and the Presbyterian Church were closest to her heart. *Book One Hilltop Lodge: Frances' Birthday Celebration*

Christmas—the music, the flowers, and overall seasonal mood. But Frances was anxious to get back to Meadow Brook Farm for her Christmas luncheon with Patrick—and thus the time seemed to drag.

Fortunately, her mother and stepfather also appeared to be conscious of the time on this particular Sunday—and kept their post-service greetings and conversation very brief. By 10:30 a.m. they were on the road back to Meadow Brook.

Afternoon

Regarding the meal—Frances had requested certain items, and Hannah had prepared an especially nice lunch basket that also included a variety of holiday pastries. These were beautiful! Frances already had some appetizers and drink choices in her Hilltop kitchen. It would be a wonderful luncheon!

Frances started a blazing fire in her fireplace. It helped to make the tree look even more festive. She also placed three wrapped packages underneath the Christmas tree. And she brought a Sander's candy package for Patrick to give to

Hank—as well as a small frosted chocolate cake that she made and boxed for him!

Patrick was very prompt—arriving at Hilltop Lodge at precisely noon. Frances, of course, repeated her usual greeting, "Happy Sunday!" and she added, "And Merry Christmas!"

She asked for his coat. She would place it in a small closet between the living and dining rooms. It was then she noticed that he was wearing clothing that she had not seen before. These were not genuine formal or dress apparel, but nor were these his usual work clothes. He was attempting to dress up for her party! She had simply worn her usual riding clothes—as she intended to take Dolly for a run after the party.

"You look quite handsome." Frances said.

Patrick smiled—but it was not his usual wide grin. "Thank you." His voice was flat. His facial expression troubled.

"Is everything okay?" Frances asked. "You seem different to me."

Standing just a few feet apart, he looked at her without changing his expression. "We need to talk."

Frances tried to lighten the situation. She queried, "Before my wonderful lunch?"

Patrick took her hand and guided her to the sofa facing the fireplace and tree.

"Frances...I don't want to upset you. So when I finish talking, let's please enjoy your holiday meal." He added, "Everything will be okay."

The final message did not register with Frances. She was alarmed at his opening sentence....that he didn't wish to upset her. What could it be? She sat with him on the sofa, and didn't say a word.

"Hank talked with me this morning. I guess that we have not been quite as clever as we thought. He is aware of our Sunday lunches, and urged us to stop meeting here at Hilltop." Patrick was relieved that he had gotten out the key message in a single breath.

Frances was stunned. And hurt. She really liked Hank. She finally angrily stammered, "Why would he be watching us so closely?"

"Frances, please don't be mad at Hank. I truly believe that he is just trying to help us. He is afraid that I might lose my job here at Meadow Brook Farm if your mother and stepfather learned about our friendship—or more accurately—our meetings."

Frances suddenly grasped the severity of the situation. Patrick needed this job. Her anger transformed into a deep sadness. "I do understand. But I will miss your friendship so very much."

"We can continue to be friends. Hank didn't see a problem with me accompanying you on your late afternoon rides." Patrick now provided Frances with a much more genuine, reassuring smile.

Frances was still very disappointed with this change, but she wanted Patrick to enjoy a Christmas party. So she took a deep breath, smiled, and said, "Let us have lunch!"

When they moved to the dining table, Patrick actually gasped. It was set with real china, crystal glasses, and Christmas linen napkins. She had carefully arranged the plates of food—with the decorated pastries placed in the center of the table. "Frances! This is just beautiful!"

They sat down together and enjoyed the meal.

Frances now took Patrick's hand and led him to the sofa. "Now it is present time for my guest of honor."

Patrick was not prepared for this portion of the afternoon party. He mumbled, "I only made you the small horse that I placed on the tree. I didn't know that we would be exchanging gifts."

"And I love the horse! I can't match your skill in making such a precious gift, but I did purchase a few items that I want you to have." Frances handed him the first gift—the Sander's chocolate package.

He laughed—saying, "I'll need to hide these from Hank. He has such a sweet tooth."

"Oh, I forgot to mention that I have two items for you to take to Hank and one item each for John and George. Of course, everyone receives a chocolate candy package. But—I also have a small chocolate cake for Hank that you told me he would want." Frances added, "Please don't reveal that I am the giver. Just find a hiding place that each will stumble into over the next day or so."

Frances then handed Patrick the gift-wrapped work gloves. It was beautiful paper. He eagerly opened the package. "Oh, gosh. These are great. I really do need new gloves. Thank you."

Finally, she handed him the gift-wrapped silver chain. This was her special present for Patrick. Again, he opened it with much enthusiasm. Frances knew that he had never opened a Christmas package before today. When he opened the black and silver velvet-lined box, he just stared at the chain. At last he murmured, "I don't know what to say."

Silence followed. So Frances offered an explanation. "I thought that you could place your holy medals on this chain rather than keeping them in your pants pocket." She added, "You won't need to worry about the chain rusting. It is real silver. And it shouldn't break while you work. It is a thick mariner chain."

Patrick looked up at her. "This is such a very generous gift. I will always wear it." And he added, "I will always remember the friend who gave it to me."

Soon it was time for Patrick to depart. He had his presents—and those for Hank. Each knew that this would be his last visit to Hilltop Lodge—and each felt a deep sadness. But they made plans to meet at the stables at four o'clock for an hour horse ride.

Frances walked back to the farm house. She still had gifts to wrap for her family. Patrick returned to the stables to work. Hank was standing outside waiting for him.

"How did it go?" Hank asked in a lowered voice.

Patrick sighed. "Okay, I guess." He offered no other information. Following an awkward silence, Patrick handed the small boxed chocolate cake and the Sander's candy package to Hank. "These are Christmas gifts from Frances." He walked into the barn and then turned suddenly to once again face Hank.

"Actually, I was instructed to hide these in a place for you to find—so that you would not know the identity of the giver. Her mother only approved her to give her nanny and teacher something. Please keep this to yourself." Patrick proceeded to the back of the barn.

Hank replied, "Thank you." And then added, "I'm sorry."

Patrick again stopped and turned to face Hank. "I know."

Late Afternoon

Frances arrived at the stables at four o'clock. Patrick had already saddled both horses. As he handed Frances the reins, she spotted immediately that Patrick was wearing the new gloves that she had bought for him.

"The gloves look good on you." Frances then stepped forward to be closer to him—reaching for the collar on Patrick's coat. She tugged on it gently—pulling it back from his neck—to reveal a portion of the new silver chain. She smiled. "This looks good, too."

Patrick also smiled. "Again, thank you."

She then turned and walked Dolly out of the barn. Patrick trailed behind her with Spirit. As always, Patrick helped Frances mount her horse before mounting his horse. And they headed toward the Meadow Brook Hall building site.

Patrick was still overwhelmed—stunned—each time he and Frances inspected the construction site. It was difficult to fathom the magnitude of the planned home.

"It will be quite beautiful." Frances interrupted his thoughts.

Patrick nodded, but said, "I doubt that I will ever see the interior."

"I <u>will</u> provide you with a tour." Frances assured him. She emphasized the word 'will'.

He gazed at Frances. So still. He didn't nod—didn't move a muscle. A blank facial expression.

She repeated, "I will provide you a tour. I promise." She then signaled Dolly to gallop toward the woods. Patrick followed.

She dismounted and led them to a small stream not far into the woods. Both Dolly and Spirit drank. Frances tied her horse to a small tree, and sat on a very large rock. She signaled for Patrick to do the same. It was nearly sunset.

"If we are quiet, we might be able to see a large herd of deer exit these woods and go into the fields in search of food." Frances whispered. "They are fun to watch as they prance and play."

Patrick sat motionless for several minutes. Finally he whispered, "I think that I hear them."

The sound of their hoofs was undeniable. Frances and Patrick stood and calmed their horses. Approximately thirty feet from where they sat by the edge of the woods, a herd of perhaps twenty-five deer traveled out into the open fields. They were so agile…graceful…beautiful. Frances watched the deer—Patrick watched Frances. She was so captivated by these creatures. Perhaps not as enamored as she was with horses, but still a childlike fascination. He envied—but admired—her passion.

"Never lose your enthusiasm…that intensity." Patrick whispered.

She turned to face him. A single tear drop fell down her left cheek. With his right gloved hand he wiped the tear from her face.

"It's growing dark. We should get back." His voice was trembling.

Frances and Patrick walked their horses out of the woods. Their sudden appearance, of course, caused the deer to run in multiple directions. They mounted and rode the horses back to the stable or main barn. Patrick helped Frances dismount her horse. As he lowered her to the ground, she scanned the area—and seeing no one—she hugged Patrick. It was brief, but robust.

"Merry Christmas." she said. Frances then began walking at a rapid pace toward the farm house.

Patrick was so surprised by her sudden embrace—he simply stood there watching her disappear down the hill.

Evening

Frances only had fifteen minutes to prepare for dinner. Mother didn't approve of her riding clothes being worn at the evening meal, so she quickly changed outfits. She was the last family member to sit down in the dining room that evening. After exchanging customary greetings with her mother, stepfather and brother, they bowed their heads and said grace—their meal prayer. As always, Hannah had prepared a delicious feast.

Following dinner, Frances sat in the parlor. She had brought a book that she intended to read over the Christmas holiday, but she simply sat and stared out the bay window. Snowflakes were softly falling. It was peaceful to watch. She reflected on the day's events…both the ups and downs. She was so disappointed to learn that she and Patrick's secret Sunday lunches were not secret—and that these clandestine meetings would now end. But she did enjoy her first Christmas party in her Hilltop Lodge. She wanted Patrick to experience a special Christmas—and he seemed genuinely appreciative—and impressed—by her preparations. He gasped when he viewed the table setting. It was beautiful. And he obviously approved of the meal—eating everything that was set out. It was delicious. And, finally, Frances felt certain that she had chosen the right gifts…the best gifts for him. He so needed the work gloves—and so wanted the silver chain. Of course, the Sanders chocolates were an obvious choice. Frances smiled at this last thought—as her family had been joking about these chocolates over the past month.

"Frances...here you are!" Mrs. Dodge Wilson interrupted her daughter's reflections.

Frances stood and walked to her mother. As she embraced her—she thought of her earlier embrace of Patrick—and his apparent shock at her actions. She found this to be amusing.

"I was going to read, but it was so nice to just sit and watch the snowfall." Frances then asked, "Did you need me for something?"

Mrs. Dodge Wilson responded, "John is at the front door. He was concerned because there were lights on in your Hilltop Lodge."

"I'm sorry, I must have forgotten to turn the lights off when I finished my lunch this afternoon." She added, "I was in a bit of a hurry to ride Dolly."

"No problem. I'll loan John my key to turn off the lights."

"Mother—would you mind if I accompanied John to Hilltop? I haven't seen my Christmas tree at night time."

"Well, if you like! But please don't linger."

John and Frances chatted along the way. She noted that he was limping a bit—but he explained that he had twisted his ankle earlier in the day. Regardless, John was in a very good mood. He was excited because his younger brother and his wife from Ohio was coming to visit for the holidays. He hadn't seen them in three years. Frances was happy for John. As they neared Hilltop, they saw a figure standing in the front of the house. Frances realized first that it was Patrick, but said nothing.

"Patrick…good evening." John greeted him. "Any problems?"

Patrick explained that he had seen the lights from the main stable, and wanted to make sure that everything was okay.

"I feel so safe here at Meadow Brook Farm!" Frances exclaimed. "Everyone is looking out for my Hilltop Lodge!"

The three laughed. John opened the door and Frances entered alone. John and Patrick remained outside talking about the change in weather. She began to turn off the interior lights. But before she turned off the living room lamp, Frances reached up and removed the small horse from her Christmas tree. She placed it deep in her coat pocket. Patrick had made it for her. She wanted to keep it with her.

When Frances exited—and John locked the door—Frances held her hand out for the key.

"John—I can walk back to the farm house alone. No problem."

John looked skeptical. He wouldn't want to anger Mrs. Wilson. But he was so close to his room in the smaller house by the stables. He was anxious to get off his feet and rest his sore ankle. Then Patrick offered his assistance.

"I can walk Frances back to the main house. I've been wanting to update her on Dolly's progress with jumping."

John accepted his offer. "Thank you, Patrick. And good night Miss Frances."

As they departed from John, Patrick proceeded to detail Dolly's improvement. When he felt certain that enough distance separated the two of them from John, he stopped. Frances also stopped.

"Is everything okay with you—with us? This afternoon after our ride—I felt that you were saying a final goodbye to me." Patrick still didn't know how to interpret her embrace. "I've been so anxious to speak alone with you."

Frances didn't realize that he would construe her brief hug as being something negative. "No. Just the opposite. I wanted you to understand that we will always be friends."

The relief on Patrick's face was clearly seen by Frances. He placed his arm around her shoulders and began leading her back to the farm house. All of the day's disappointing events just seemed to disappear with him next to her—holding her close to him.

He removed his arm as they came within the 'lighted' area of the farm house. He continued to walk with her up the porch steps to the front door. The door was unlocked. Frances opened it to find her mother waiting. Mrs. Dodge Wilson was surprised to see Patrick and not John. But Frances quickly explained about his ankle injury.

"Thank you, young man." Mrs. Dodge Wilson then added, "And please tell John that I hope that his ankle feels better in the morning."

"I will. Goodnight, Mrs. Wilson. Goodnight, Miss Frances." Patrick walked down the porch steps. In unison the mother and daughter said, "Goodnight."

Chapter 6

Christmas Day

Saturday, December 25, 1926

Morning

Very early—well before breakfast—Frances tiptoed to the staff wing of the farmhouse and placed a Sanders chocolate package outside of Anne's (the housekeeper), Hannah's (the cook) and Mary's (the nanny) bedroom doors. On Christmas Eve, she had given—in private—a wrapped book that Nanny Mary had wanted (and her mother approved). She had also given all staff a special Christmas card—also approved by her mother—the day before. But the chocolates were something extra that was secret. Of course she gave Patrick his chocolates at their special luncheon when she gave him the work gloves and silver chain. And he agreed to hide the chocolates for John (grounds/driver), George (farm hand) and Hank (stable manager). And, of course, she had given Miss Taylor, her tutor, her gifts prior to her leaving for her vacation. Today—later in the afternoon—Frances would give her family members their gifts! And last—but certainly not least in her eyes—Frances would make a trip to the stables with special treats for her horses! But first on the day's agenda was church.

Following breakfast, Frances' family bundled in their car and John drove to the Presbyterian Church for a 10 a.m. Christmas morning service. Frances' brother Danny—as expected—complained about wearing a suit, the cold weather, and the long drive. Regarding the drive, Frances judged it as being quite nice. The sun was out today—and the snow and ice on the trees and in the fields sparkled like diamonds. The effect was beautiful.

The service was also enjoyable. The minister was very positive—very cheery. The music was joyful. And the church itself was adorned with festive wreaths, fresh flowers (including a multitude of poinsettias and carnations) and a large decorated Christmas tree. (Frances had a certain affinity for Christmas trees that she couldn't explain!) At the conclusion of the service, the congregation crowded into the Friendship Hall where there was a delicious fruit punch with sherbet ice cream and a huge assortment of homemade Christmas cookies and pastries. Danny was happy for the first time today.

Mr. and Mrs. Wilson chatted with a number of church members. Danny ate. Frances watched. She found it interesting to observe others—their mannerisms, facial expressions, tone of voice. She also listened carefully to the content of their conversation. Her mother, of course, talked about the planning and construction of Meadow Brook Hall. She appreciated any audience—and today her church friends were particularly mesmerized by her description of the planned estate. Her verbal blueprint was indeed captivating.

The family remained at the church until eleven o'clock. They would be arriving back home just a bit late for lunch, but Mrs. Dodge Wilson had forewarned the staff to expect a late return. It was Christmas Day!

Afternoon

Danny found it particularly difficult to sit still during lunch. He desperately wanted to open the family presents. His mother had locked the parlor doors—where the Christmas tree and gifts were awaiting the proper time—just to insure that he would not take an early peek. Frances was also anxious, but was much more patient than her younger brother.

"Frances, you seem to be very calm today. Aren't you curious about your presents?" Mrs. Dodge Wilson asked.

Frances beamed. "Oh, yes, I am very curious!" And then looking directly at her brother, she said, "But I really do enjoy the anticipation."

Danny stuck out his tongue at his sister—which prompted an immediate admonishment from his mother.

"Daniel. We do not stick out our tongues at anyone." Mrs. Dodge Wilson scolded. "It isn't nice."

The young boy of nine then apologized to his sister and lunch proceeded.

Later in the afternoon—following lunch—the family gathered in the parlor around the grand 14-foot Christmas tree. Mrs. Dodge Wilson had spared no expense in her purchase of numerous ornaments for the tree. As Frances sat next to Danny on the floor—they wanted to be close to the tree and gifts—she admired her mother's handiwork. It really was a breathtaking tree. But Frances still felt that her Hilltop Lodge tree was equal in beauty—perhaps a different kind of beauty—but still a splendor to enjoy.

Each family member took a turn opening a gift. This was the first year that Frances had done her own shopping and wrapping of presents. Frances was proud of her efforts. Her mother fawned over the short story that Frances had written for her about Hilltop Lodge. And she was happily surprised with the large photography book on European architecture. Her stepfather was also pleased with his book about agriculture—as well as the much needed winter hat, scarf and lined gloves. (Michigan winters are cold!) Danny squealed in delight when he opened the Lincoln Logs and Tinkertoys that Frances had purchased for him. And, of course, each family member received Sanders chocolates from Frances!

Frances and Danny's parents—and Santa Claus—had gifted them with items that they so wanted! For Danny—his mother and stepfather gave him the fire engine and the Coaster wagon that he wanted. And Santa brought him the Lionel train set with all of the extras. For Frances—she received new riding outfits and boots from her mother and step-father. And Santa brought her a magnificent saddle. Frances was anxious to ride Dolly with the new saddle.

At the conclusion of the gift opening, Frances' stepfather gave a brief speech to the family. He began with a prayer—thanking God for his family and home. He then spoke to his wife, stepdaughter and stepson about how fortunate they were—and how important it was to share with others. He mentioned that he and Mrs. Dodge Wilson had given generously to both their church and to the Salvation Army (a particular favorite charity of Mrs. Dodge Wilson)—as well as gifting each Meadow Brook farm staff member with a Christmas cash bonus earlier this morning.

Evening

Dinner would be a little later than usual due to all of the day's festivities. Hannah had been instructed to begin serving at 7 o'clock. Frances had convinced her parents to allow her to visit the stables prior to dinner. She told them that she wanted to bring her horses some extra special treats! And—most importantly—she was anxious to try on Dolly's new saddle. John—who was present because he had dropped by to give Mr. Wilson the receipt for a new light pole installed at the end of the gravel driveway—graciously volunteered to walk with Frances and carry the saddle. It was, after all, a bit heavy.

"Fine." Her mother had agreed to the plan, but added, "It will be dark upon your return. It's nearly five o'clock now. So—please ask either Hank or Patrick to walk you back to the house."

This was the first time that Frances had heard her mother use Patrick's name. She had always referred to him as "that new young man" or as "Hank's helper". But, of course, Patrick had only been employed at Meadow Brook Farm a short time—just one month. So it was understandable that Mrs. Dodge Wilson was not yet very familiar with him. Also, she was definitely preoccupied with the planning of Meadow Brook Hall.

Frances decided to tease her mother just a bit about having an escort. "Of course—if it will make you more comfortable." Frances sighed. She nodded her head up and down—showing that she agreed with her mother's concerns. "I suppose that there could be some dangerous deer lurking about."

Her mother responded with a sarcastic "Ha, ha." She added, "I am a mother—and mothers are permitted to worry excessively about their children."

Well—Frances thought—how does one argue with that logic?

Frances dressed warmly. She and John headed for the stables with her carrying a sack of special treats for her horses and John carrying the new saddle. Patrick was just outside the main barn when he saw the two approaching. He quickly moved toward them.

"Merry Christmas!" Patrick then asked, "What have we here?"

Frances quickly spoke up. "Santa gifted me with this beautiful new saddle."

Patrick began inspecting it. He concluded, "A real beauty." As he started to lift it—he said, "John—I'll take that saddle from you. It must weigh 30 or 40 pounds." He smiled at Frances—a mischievous smile.

"It is only 22 pounds." Frances corrected him. "But you are correct—it is a beauty!"

John bid the two good night after insuring that Patrick would walk Frances back to the farm house. They parted just outside the barn door.

Patrick then entered the stable carrying the new saddle. Frances walked behind him. They headed for Dolly and Duke's stalls towards the back.

"Do you want to try it on Dolly tonight?" he asked. "Do you plan to ride now?"

Frances thought for a moment before answering. "No…I don't think that I'll ride. I don't want to return too late. The family is having Christmas dinner at 7 o'clock." She added, "But I told my mother that I wanted to try on the new saddle. Do you mind helping me?"

"Not at all." Patrick lifted the saddle in place. Together they worked on the straps.

Frances stood back to admire her gift. "It really is beautiful."

"Yes—although not quite as beautiful as its owner." Patrick stared at Frances.

Frances looked down—and then behind her—as if she was making sure that no one else was present.

"We are alone." Patrick spoke up. He clasped both of her hands. "I want to thank you again—not just for the Christmas gifts—but this morning I was given an envelope that contained a cash bonus. You are a beautiful person to help me like this."

Frances quickly responded, "But that was from my mother and stepfather. Really, I had nothing to do with the cash bonus."

"But you did." Patrick seemed certain that she had helped. He explained. "Hank told me that he talked to Mr. Wilson—that he asked that I be given a bonus even though I was new at Meadow Brook Farm. And I believe that he did so because of you." Patrick emphasized those final words.

Frances was perplexed. "Because of me?" she repeated.

"Hank is very fond of you. He worries so much about you because of the loss of your father, uncle and sister in such a short time span." Patrick continued. "He says that you seem so much happier now. I guess he believes that this has something to do with me."

Frances was dumbstruck. And then Patrick asked, "Does it have something to do with me?"

She was blindsided by such a direct question. She was so startled that words just wouldn't come out of her mouth. It seemed as if she had lost all muscle control. She accidentally dropped her bag of treats to the barn floor. Struggling—she finally whispered a single word. "Yes." she said.

Patrick then kissed her on the forehead—and then embraced her. It seemed like they stood there—in front of Dolly's stall together in a strong embrace—for at least five minutes. When he released her, he stooped and picked up her bag of treats.

"Some of these are for Duke, too?" he asked.

Frances nodded yes. Patrick began splitting up the treats—which both horses thoroughly enjoyed. He then turned to Frances, "Let me walk you back to the farmhouse now." Again, she simply nodded yes.

As he did previously, Patrick placed his arm around her shoulders. "To help keep you warm." he said.

Halfway to the house—Frances stopped. "Patrick, I want you to understand that you do a wonderful job here at Meadow Brook. I just can't take the credit for you receiving a cash bonus."

He looked at Frances as though he was seeing her for the first time. "You really are a true friend—a beautiful person. So I'll share something with you—but you must promise me that you will not try to help me anymore—because now the situation is resolved."

Again, Frances was perplexed. But she agreed by saying, "I promise."

"This bonus means so much to me because my sister needs some help. And now I can help her." Patrick said no more.

Frances smiled. And then she stretched on her tiptoes and kissed Patrick on his left cheek—whispered, "Merry Christmas"—and then embraced him as he had embraced her in the stables. She released him after only a minute, but the message was clear. She also regarded Patrick as a true friend—a beautiful person.

Frances was quiet during dinner—but smiled at the appropriate times when her mother, stepfather or brother made an amusing comment or clever observation. Now that the Christmas festivities were over—she was concentrating on welcoming in 1927. Yes—New Years was just a week away. Of course, she was also absorbed in thoughts about Patrick.

Her mother interrupted these thoughts. "Frances? Are you with us?"

The question jolted Frances a bit—but she recovered quickly. "Yes! I was just thinking about the arrival of 1927. How will we celebrate the New Year?"

"Well—your stepfather and I just planned on staying at home with you and Danny!" her mother replied. "Perhaps we could play cards or games?"

Frances nodded. "That could be fun."

"I have both the Touring and the Pit card games." Mr. Wilson offered.

It was settled. The family would be playing games on New Year's Eve!

It was now eleven o'clock. Frances lay in bed wide awake reflecting on the happenings of the past few years—the past few weeks—and of the past few hours. She concluded that the Christmas holiday of 1926 was really quite wonderful. For the first time—in a very long time—she felt genuinely happy. She pondered on her new—and growing interest—in horses. Her mother and stepfather fully supported this budding passion. Since moving to Meadow Brook Farm, they bought her two of her own horses—as well as four other pedigree or thoroughbred horses. They enlarged the stables—and hired two staff to help manage the stables. And, of course, this Christmas they gifted her with a premium saddle and riding boots.

And in November—for her twelfth birthday—they had gifted her with Hilltop Lodge. Mrs. Dodge Wilson had some very practical reasons for this extravagant birthday present. She wanted Frances to learn the art of keeping a house—of being a hostess—and of budgeting. (Yes—Frances actually had her own checking account at the age of twelve. Mrs. Dodge Wilson had made special arrangements with their bank.) Her mother wanted Frances to prosper and triumph in her social world—and she felt that Hilltop Lodge could provide the real-life experiences to help ensure her daughter's success. It was not really designed to be a 'playhouse' for Frances, but rather a setting where she could learn the skills of managing a household. But for Frances—it was so much more. She loved having her own special place. Frances felt very safe, very secure there. It was her hideaway—her private retreat.

Of course, the most evident or obvious change to her family's life was that of their impending residence—Meadow Brook Hall. The discussion and planning occupied a great deal of her mother's time—and her mother wished for Frances to be fully aware of the ongoing work being done. It was exciting—actually a bit overwhelming. Frances often felt as Patrick did when she told him that it would be 88,000 square feet in size—speechless. The girl who America would later dub a "Princess"—would live in a mansion that would be called "America's Castle". *In a little less than three years—on November 19, 1929—Mrs. Dodge Wilson would host a gathering of over 800 guests attending the lavish housewarming party for Meadow Brook Hall. This party took place just three weeks following the stock market crash that led to the Great Depression. These were two very different worlds.*

In addition to horses and Hilltop Lodge and Meadow Brook Hall, Frances pondered on the significant changes in her family over the past year. She thought about her mother and her Aunt Anna who had both lost their husbands six years back (in 1920) but now each had remarried this past year. (Her mother in June of 1925 and her aunt in May of 1926.) Frances still missed her father—and her uncle—but her stepfather was very kind and loving to both her and Danny. And he and her mother seemed so contented. And her Aunt Anna—as well—seemed happy with her new husband---Mr. Dillman—who Frances found to be charming and fun.

Frances also reflected on the loss of her sister approximately four years following the death of her father. Anna (named after their Aunt Anna) died from complications of measles. Of course, this time period was perhaps hardest on her mother. People say that the loss of a child is the worst. But the death of Anna also had a profound effect on Frances. She considered her sister to be her best friend. She became withdrawn after her sister's death. She struggled between feelings of intense anger and deep sadness. She had no interest in anything. But now she had a new best friend—Patrick.

Patrick shared with her the early loss of a parent—at the young and tender age of five. Frances had lost her father and Patrick had lost his mother. But Patrick also suffered from the consequences of an alcoholic father who did not work regularly. He and his sister and brother lived in severe poverty—as well as being separated and shifted from various relatives' or friends' homes who would care for them for a limited amount of time when their father simply disappeared. When he would reappear, it was not necessarily any better for the three children—except that they could reunite if even for a brief amount of time.

When Frances first met Patrick, he had left his family's small farm in Milford and began walking—with Detroit being his ultimate goal. That was in October. He was only fourteen years of age—but looked older. He was tall—which helped. He wanted to find a job, and heard that Detroit was a city of opportunity. He planned to tell prospective employers that he was eighteen years of age. But when the winter set in early in Michigan—and he became ill—he sought shelter in an abandoned small work shed along the way. This shelter was located on property that was part of Meadow Brook Farm in Rochester. Hank found him—took pity on the young man—and brought him food, water and blankets. As he recovered—Patrick worked hard to help Hank with the new stables. Hank was impressed by Patrick's knowledge about the care of horses. Patrick also explored the farm and its 1,500 acres—including Hilltop Lodge. Of course, he and Frances crossed paths—and became fast friends. (The full story of their meeting is found in Book One.)[16]

Frances felt fortunate that Patrick had entered her life—a life that had been very sheltered—but one that also held great promise for the future. She no longer dwelled on the loss of her father, sister and uncle. She learned empathy for others who experienced similar hardships in life. She appreciated their struggles and vowed to conquer her own. Frances was determined to focus on a new path, and Patrick continually encouraged her to do so. Yes—Frances Dodge would race horses!

The hour was late. Frances yawned. She pulled the blankets up to her chin. She closed her eyes and dreamed. Frances Dodge—a forthcoming internationally famous horsewoman.

END

[16] *Book One Hilltop Lodge: Frances' Birthday Celebration*